Ruled By Destiny

11-12-2014

Enjoy reading Ruth

Love
Linda Newton

Ruled By Destiny

Linda M. Newton

authorHOUSE®

AuthorHouse™
1663 Liberty Drive
Bloomington, IN 47403
www.authorhouse.com
Phone: 1-800-839-8640

First published by AuthorHouse   07/27/2011

ISBN: 978-1-4634-4330-6 (sc)
ISBN: 978-1-4634-4329-0 (dj)
ISBN: 978-1-4634-4328-3 (ebk)

Library of Congress Control Number: 2011913172

Printed in the United States of America

Any people depicted in stock imagery provided by Thinkstock are models, and such images are being used for illustrative purposes only.
Certain stock imagery © Thinkstock.

This book is printed on acid-free paper.

This book is dedicated to my lovely daughter, Rachel McKenna Newton

and

to my beloved sister, Diane Marie Juneau.

Life with her may be short but her memory will always be in my heart.

Chapter One

Lone Wolf guided his horse down the mountainside, weaving in and out of the trees. He stopped to lean forward to whisper to his horse, Thunder, "What is it?" Thunder had been with him in many battles and knew when something wasn't right. Slowly, Lone Wolf reached down for his bow, notching an arrow. He was ready to defend himself and his horse. He caught a glimpse of a horse and rider and, hearing a familiar bird call and looking more closely, saw that it was his best friend of many years, Laughing Otter.

Still grinning, Lone Wolf lowered his bow. "Are you wishing to go to the Great Spirit before your time?"

Laughing Otter chuckled. "It's not like you could hit me from there." Grinning from ear to ear he rode up to Lone Wolf. "If only you were that good of a shot I might have something to worry about, but we both know you're not."

Otter had a point, but Lone Wolf had hit him once before. He may have been aiming for the apple in Otter's hand, but he had hit Otter all the same. Growing up together they were more like brothers than best friends.

"So how was your vision quest? You have been gone for days now. I thought you might have forgotten your way back home," Laughing Otter said.

Lone Wolf grunted his reply as they turned their horses and started down the familiar trail leading the way home. Laughing Otter was known as one who would not let issues drop, but this time he kept a silent tongue.

Lone Wolf's father, Chief Two Timbers, wanted the neighboring tribes to join forces as one. It had all started late last month when Chief Two Timbers was approached by Chief White Cloud wanting to arrange a marriage between his daughter Willow and Lone Wolf. It wasn't that Willow was a complete stranger, and she was nice on the eyes and would make a good wife. Lone Wolf would also be chief over both tribes. But there just wasn't that spark that he knew he should have for her.

1

They continued to ride in silence, each deep in his own thoughts. Lone Wolf did not quite know how to explain to his friend the white woman he had come across the first day he was on his quest. He had been riding his horse following the river when he heard soft humming along with a splash of water. He got off his horse and tied it up to graze. He started on foot, gently approaching the river, and crouched down, ducking between the smaller trees. He dropped down behind the great ferns next to the river to look, with knife in hand in case of danger. There she was bathing in the water looking like a water spirit, her blonde hair floating beside her as she floated on her back with her arms moving by her side. Her breasts were saluting with raised nipples that puckered as the gentle wind caressed them. She just continued to float on the water effortlessly. His mouth suddenly went dry, and his heart started to beat faster. Then she lifted her head up out of the water, her knees going under her until her feet touched the bottom of the river. Lone Wolf did not even breathe; he just continued to stare. He watched as she stood up and walked over to a large boulder to grab her soap. She lathered her body, turned from the boulder, and then plunged headfirst into the water to rinse off, with her bottom coming to the surface to peek up at him. Lone Wolf's stomach knotted. His manhood stirred, taking on a life of its own. Remembering the knife he was still holding, he put it away. His water spirit now finished bathing and started walking toward the bank of the river. Her beautiful naked body glowed while her hair dripped with water, and she suddenly stopped and turned her head in his direction until her green eyes were looking right at him. Lone Wolf did not even dare to blink.

"Selena! Selena!" a young voice called out. "Where are you?" The white girl turned away, her attention distracted, toward the voice calling her name. She grabbed a piece of cloth to wipe the excess water off her body. She knew that her younger brother Reid was calling. Her mother must have sent him to tell her that it was time to come home. Selena scrambled into her clothes and pulled her hair into a ponytail while running down the trail. Lone Wolf remained in his hiding place. He did not even dare to breathe, as he did not want to been seen. However, Selena slowed down her pace and turned around, looking. Something was different. The hairs on the back of her neck stood up, and she had the feeling that she was being watched.

Taking Lone Wolf out of his memories, Laughing Otter said, "You don't have to tell me, but you look like you are thinking way too hard."

Lone Wolf turned to his friend, noticing for the first time that they were entering the outskirts of their village. "Tell you what?" he asked.

Laughing Otter grunted, thinking to himself about what had his friend so occupied. *I guess he will speak when he is ready.*

Both men dismounted, leading their horses over to the young braves who were the pony watchers and leaving their horses in their care. Strong and tall, they walked through the village until they noticed that they were being surrounded by little children. Lone Wolf could feel a gentle tug on his leg. "Did you bring anything back?" Looking down, he could see a sea of little faces looking up at him. He removed the leather bag that he had been carrying and placed it gently on the ground, bent down, and opened it. All the children were gathered around him trying to get a peek into the opening. "What is it? What's in the pouch?" The little voices asked. Suddenly a small nose poked out; next came two little black eyes and a set of paws that finally come over the edge of the pouch.

"Oh! Can I hold it? Is it a puppy?" Harlow asked, her child's eyes shining brightly.

Lone Wolf replied, "It's not a puppy. It is a young wolf pup, and he is free to come and go as the pup wants. He has been separated from his pack, so he will join our family." Lone Wolf shot them a look, warning them to be nice to the pup.

Lone Wolf took the little pup gently out and placed him on the ground. The pup looked around and sniffed the ground while licking a couple of wiggly toes. Soon laughter erupted into screams of delight. However, before the many little hands could grab for him or scoop him up he was off and running as fast as his little legs could carry him. Following behind in hot pursuit was a group of giggling children.

Watching the pup run off, the men continued walking until they reached the center of the village. Lone Wolf noticed his mother Lilly sitting next to a fire by his parents' tipi. He saw her in her doeskin dress, her long black hair braided and her eyes dark brown with fine lines at the corners that only showed when she smiled. He noticed that she was putting beads on a new doeskin dress she was making. Lone Wolf thought to himself that it must be the dress she planned to wear to the marriage ceremony.

His mother looked up from her beadwork. She brushed several strands of hair out of her eyes. A gentle smile played across her face. "I see you found our wayward cub," she said to Otter.

"Good luck getting him to talk," Otter said. "It seems that his vision has robbed him of his tongue."

By the look on her son's face she could tell he was not ready to share yet. "Sit down; it has been a long journey." She motioned for both men to be seated. "I have rabbit stew and flatbread ready to come off the fire." Lilly entered the tipi, retrieved a couple of wooden bowls, and ladled in the steaming stew. She handed each a bowl with flatbread, and they ate like there was no tomorrow, and the silence was loud when unanswered questions hung in the air.

She picked mindlessly at the strand she had been about to bead. "Your father is out scouting," she said, breaking the silence.

"Has there been trouble while I was gone?"

"No," Laughing Otter and Lilly answered in unison.

Laughing Otter looked at Lone Wolf. Lilly kept glancing toward him too.

Lone Wolf realized that he wasn't going to get any peace until he told them what had been shown in his vision. He looked at his mother, who had just beaded the same bead twice, and then at his friend, who was wiping the stew from his chin. He knew that they both wondered what had been shown to him by the spirits.

Lone Wolf looked at them both. "Do you want to hear of my vision?" He knew that he had their attention now; they both nodded their heads, not saying a word. "I went to my place of safety to pray and fast for three days. On the evening of the third day, I was sitting on the ground as the sun was setting. I sat with legs crossed and my eyes closed in a meditative state when I suddenly felt the presence of warmth next to me." Looking at them both he saw that they were listening to his every word. "With my eyes still closed I could see a vision of a large dark wolf running with his pack. The wolf was not the leader yet but looked to be next in line."

Lilly thought to herself, *Well, that would be Lone Wolf and his father Two Timbers.* She nodded her head so her son would continue; she wanted to hear the rest.

"In my vision there came another pack of wolves, and they mingled together. Surrounding a willow tree both groups were on edge, snipping and snapping, all the while circling around this tree. Suddenly a colorful bird flew through the air to land on a branch of the willow tree. It looked down at the dark wolf." He could see Laughing Otter's eyebrows move together with a question, but he remained silent.

"I have never seen this type of bird before. It had many colors of blue and green and long feathers with the shape of eyes at the end of the tail feathers. The dark wolf jumped at the tree, but the colorful bird flew down with no fear. The willow tree branches drooped as in defeat. The dark wolf walked off along with the colorful bird balancing on his back.

"Just as the vision started to fade, I heard the sorrowful cry of a wolf. It came from the warmth next to me." Lone Wolf looked at them both; his mother, he could tell, was rethinking the story in her mind, placing all the pieces together to figure out the meaning.

Laughing Otter picked up another piece of flatbread, one a little on the hefty side, and bit off a piece and chewed, deep in thought.

Lone Wolf fixed them each with a gaze. "Well, you wanted to know. Now what do you think?"

Lilly spoke her words wisely. "You are in line to take your father's place when the time comes." She looked right at her son. "I see Willow, who is the daughter of Chief White Cloud from our neighboring village. I see his daughter Willow as the tree. What I do not understand is this colorful bird. I have never seen nor heard of the likes of such bird, so I am not sure what that was all about; only time will tell." Lilly continued to move her lips as she repeated her words slowly and softly, more to herself than out loud.

Laughing Otter suddenly burped and then grinned with mischief, ready to offer words of wisdom. "Well, if you ask me"—he looked at them both—"I would say that you had been dropped on your head as a baby."

Lone Wolf threw a playful punch, but Otter rolled away, laughing. For such a big guy, Otter sure could move.

"Looks like I will be moving on now," Laughing Otter said as he stood up to go to his own home.

Lone Wolf looked to his mother. "They should have named him Laughing Fool."

Lilly replied, "Did you expect anything less from him?"

Sensing that her son was still unsettled, she asked, "Lone Wolf, what is the problem? Are you not thinking of marrying Willow?"

"I've known her since I was six." Lone Wolf tapped his chest. "It just doesn't feel right in here."

"It is usually standard practice among leaders." She placed her hand on his. "Your father and I joined together the same way. We have shared many happy seasons together."

Lone Wolf shook his head, not quite sure how to reply, but he didn't have to. A bundle of gray fur ran up and crawled into his lap. The wolf laid its head on his bent knee.

"This pup came to me after the vision faded."

"I'm sure he is hungry. Give him what is left of the rabbit carcass."

Lone Wolf got up and retrieved the carcass. He gave it to the wolf, which started to chew on it. "I guess he is hungry. He looks worn out and tired from playing with the children today."

"That he does. Your father should be coming soon. Did you want to stay to speak with him?" Lilly asked.

Lone Wolf knew that his father, whom he loved, would ask more intense questions than his mother had. Now was the time to make a quick retreat. Standing up, he kissed his mother on her forehead, "I'm going to go on my way. Tell father that I will speak with him tomorrow."

Lone Wolf stepped over the beaded dress and headed toward his tipi. It lay on the outskirts of the village. His station as the chief's son would allow him to be closer to the middle of the village despite his young age, but he liked having a bit of distance from his family. He also preferred the company of the men his age over the elders whose tipis lay toward the center. Besides, his father always told him that in order to lead men, you must first show them that you are one of them.

The village was starting to settle down. He could see the community fire and hear the drums beating and soft chanting, but he didn't feel like joining in tonight. He had too much on his mind. He entered his dark and cool tipi. His bedding was to one side with furs to sleep on. Everything was as he had left it. The wolf pup followed him, dragging what was left of the rabbit carcass between his legs.

"Come on, Wolf, put that down. You have had enough." Wolf looked at him and lay down stretched out on his belly, his head cocked to one side with his ears facing his new master. He continued to chew on the leftover rabbit. "Well, I'm going to bed," he told his new furry friend. "Try to keep the chewing down, would you?"

Lying down with his arms under his head, Lone Wolf couldn't help but stare at the stars shining brightly from the top of the tipi, thinking to himself that he had left out one important part of his vision today. He had come across another creature with green eyes the same color as the feathers of the colorful bird that had showed up in his vision. He needed to see her again. Her green eyes made his stomach knot up and his palms sweat. That hadn't even happened when he went into his first battle. Willow was a sweet girl and had a beautiful body, and the two tribes joined as one would be very powerful. She just didn't have the connection that he felt with this white girl named Selena.

He felt the wolf pup curl up by the bottom of his feet. That was the last thought he had as he drifted off to sleep.

Chapter Two

———

Selena lay in bed remembering when she was at the river bathing the other day. She had felt that someone had been watching her but couldn't see or tell if there was anyone there. Her father would be furious if he knew. He didn't like her going to the river by herself. He was a fair man but still protective over his children. He just wanted what was best for them all. Changes had been happening in the area with the many new settlers moving in. The natives had been restless of late, with more and more of their land being settled on. Rumor had it that only a day's ride from their homestead a farmhouse had been set on fire. No one was hurt, but it made everyone uneasy. Suddenly her heart quickened its pace just thinking about tomorrow when she was to ride into town. She couldn't wait. Her best friend Katie, who was also her cousin, was going to spend the week with her. After chores she was going to take her to the river, where there was a new rope to swing into the water with. Even if they had to sneak there they would be going.

"Selena, would you stop twisting and turning? You keep shaking the bed," Amy, who was only a pillow away, grumbled to her.

"Sorry. I just can't seem to get comfortable or fall asleep."

Amy turned on her side. She had long blonde hair too, but it was braided, and her nightcap was securely on her head. Her eyes were brown like their father's, and her smile mirrored his. Amy was the more soft-spoken of the two, willing to trust with no questions asked. Selena always felt that her sister was closer to their younger brother Reid, who was ten. They had a special bond. Maybe it was that they were closer in age. Amy was only twelve, but Selena felt that she could be more mature at times than her age dictated.

"Okay. I know when something is wrong. Give it up. What is the matter?" Amy asked.

"Nothing. I'm just excited for tomorrow. We get to go into town, and Pa said I could ride Spirit while he takes the family in the wagon. He is always worried that I will get into trouble or come across the natives. Just because there has been friction here and there doesn't mean it will happen to me. Pa has to realize that I'm not a child anymore."

"Yeah, I don't know why I can't ride into town on my horse with you," Amy pouted.

"You're not going to be sixteen now, are you? You're only twelve; that's why you can't ride with me," Selena told her.

"Stop changing the subject. What is wrong?"

"Shhh! You're going to wake Ma and Pa. They're downstairs—they just went to bed," Selena whispered. "Why do you think something is wrong?"

"Well, you usually fall asleep as we are saying our nightly prayers; you finish before me almost every night. Tonight you have been tossing and turning, and I don't hear any snoring coming from you."

Selena jabbed her with her elbow, making her point. "I don't snore!"

"Ouch! You do too snore," Amy replied.

"Girls, be quite up there! It's time to go to sleep. We need to get up early," they heard their pa yell from the bedroom below. They slept in the loft upstairs, and their parents had the bedroom downstairs. Reid was in a smaller room next to their parents.

Selena whispered to Amy, who was getting tired, "I can't wait to go tomorrow, because Katie gets to come back with us. Uncle Abe and Aunt Henrietta said she didn't have to work in the store tomorrow. She is going to be able to bring her horse too."

Amy lay on her back, still not sure if Selena was telling the truth or not. "Well, close your eyes and stop wiggling. I'm tired. I just want to go to sleep."

"Sorry Amy. Good night."

"Good night, Selena." The girls settled down, and deep even breathing could be heard as sleep came quickly, as did the morning.

From her sleep Selena could hear her name being called out: "Selena, Amy!" Opening her eyes she could tell her mom making breakfast. Amy was up and getting dressed. Selena yawned. It was warmer in their bed, but she could still feel the chill in the air. Selena pushed the blankets back, and her feet touched the cool floor as she climbed out of bed.

"I'm going to go feed the chickens and gather the eggs," Amy told Selena as she climbed down the ladder that led to the main room. Selena quickly dressed, brushed her hair, and then climbed down.

"Good morning, Ma." Selena greeted her mother with a peck on the cheek. "What do you want me to make this morning?"

"You can start with the flapjacks. I almost have the bacon fried. Your father is tending to the barn with your brother. Amy is feeding and gathering the eggs." Carolyn nodded her head in the direction of the flour.

Selena heard the door open, and in came her pa with her brother along with a burst of fresh morning air. They each had an armful of wood. Amy followed behind with an apron full of chicken eggs.

"Amy, take the eggs and get them in a container ready to take with us to give to your Aunt Henrietta to sell at the store."

Charles bent to put the logs next to the fireplace as Reid put his armful of wood by the cook stove.

"Breakfast is almost done, and there is fresh water in the basin for you both to wash up." Carolyn looked at Charles and Reid. Amy finished setting the table after the eggs were cleaned. Everyone knew the routine, and in no time at all everything was in place.

As they sat at the table, heads bowed, Charles said the blessing. "Amen" was repeated by all when he finished.

Charles turned to Selena. "So, you are going to ride Spirit in today?"

"Yes, Pa."

"Carolyn,"—he looked to his wife—"is Katie coming back with us today?" He took a bite of flapjack.

"Yes, she is. Henrietta told me last Sunday that she could bring her horse if she is going to be staying."

"I'm going to Grandma and Grandpa's if Katie is coming over," Reid chimed in. "'Cause Amy has to sleep in my bed, and I don't want to sleep on the floor."

Charles grinned as he ruffled his hair. "Finish your milk; let's get the horses hitched up so we can head out."

"Amy, Selena, you need to clean up. I'm going to change, and then we will be ready to go." Carolyn headed into her bedroom.

Selena rode Spirit in front of the wagon. Oh, finally freedom! The wind was blowing in her face. Most of her childhood friends were courting to be married to local men, but not Selena. She was going to be different someway or somehow. She was going to make a difference; she wasn't one to just go with the flow. Her parents might think she should just settle down and raise a family close to home, but she wasn't ready for that. Hearing the clip clop of the hooves behind her she was reminded that her pa was following behind in the wagon with the rest of the family. There weren't that many people in town, and a one-way dirt road led the way into Red Fern Valley. Selena dismounted in front of the store, tied up Spirit, and ran up the stairs. She opened the door and rushed inside. "Hello, Uncle Abe. Is Katie here?"

Her uncle was standing behind the counter, a tall man with dark hair that he had combed over. It was thinning, and she could see his scalp where the comb had gone through. Uncle Abe looked at her over his half eyeglasses. "She will be down in a minute. Did your folks come with you?"

"Yes, Uncle Abe, but I rode Spirit in. Pa let me come ahead when we hit the outskirts of town," Selena told him as she walked around looking at all of the different items her uncle had. Most of all she liked the different bonnets. "Oh, Uncle Abe, when did you get this new one?"

"A couple of days ago a peddling man came into town with a wagon full of goods. He came by and we did some trading. Aunt Henrietta liked the hat. Go ahead, Selena. Try it on."

"Oh, I don't know." She touched the rim of the hat. It was black with beautiful colorful green and blue feathers. "What kind of feathers are these? I haven't seen them before," she asked as she was inspecting the colors of the hat.

"The peddling man said they were peacock feathers around the rim."

Selena took the hat from where it was sitting and placed it on her head.

"That looks good on you, Selena. Take a look in the mirror." Uncle Abe licked the tip of his pencil and continued to do paperwork, writing down figures.

Selena walked over to a small mirror hanging on the wall with her chin down. Slowly moving her chin up, she glanced into the mirror and gasped. The hat looked great on her and would be perfect to wear to church or a barn dance. Her green-colored eyes stood out even more than usual; looking back at her was a young woman and not a child anymore.

"Oh my. That hat looks wonderful on you." Selena would have recognized that voice anywhere. She turned to Katie, who was at the bottom of the stairs, smiling as always. Katie wasn't as tall as Selena. She had dark brown eyes like Amy, but Katie had beautiful long brown hair that was thick with a natural curl; it was her best feature.

"Hi Katie." Selena took the hat off, and a slight blush tinged her cheeks. "I was waiting for you to come down. Your pa said I could try it on."

"It looks great on you. You should get it," Katie told her.

Selena shook her head wistfully, putting the hat back on the shelf.

"I would like to buy it, but it is three dollars. That would take me years to save up." She heard the rest of the family come in. Aunt Henrietta, who was always dressed nicely, was greeting everyone. Uncle Abe was shaking hands with her pa, and Amy was showing the prize eggs she had collected. Aunt Henrietta was looking at them as if they were gold. Reid was eyeing the candy containers. Uncle Abe must have snuck him a piece, because he was chewing and smiling from ear to ear.

Suddenly two gunshots exploded outside their door.

Uncle Abe took off his apron and peeked out the window. Charles was right beside him. "What in tarnation is going on?" he asked.

Aunt Henrietta whispered as she ushered Carolyn into the kitchen for tea, "Come on; let's go into the kitchen. It will be safer in there." Reid was unsure of what to do, to stay with the men or follow his mother. He chose his mother.

Selena had a different idea. She grabbed Katie by her hand, and they headed out the back door. "Come on, Katie. Let's see what is going on!"

"Selena, are you crazy? I know you do crazy things, but we don't know who is out there."

Against her better judgment, Katie headed out the back door to follow Selena, and they crouched low going around the front corner of the store. Tied to the post was Spirit, who was pulling hard to get free. He looked white-eyed and nervous with all the commotion going on.

"I don't think it's a good idea to be out here," Katie said.

"Well, go back in. I'm going to get Spirit before a stray bullet hits him."

Yanking on Selena's arm, Katie looked her right in the eyes, "You are going to get yourself shot. Your pa will tan your hide if you go out there."

It didn't stop Selena. She shook Katie's hand off and crouched down, creeping toward her horse.

Katie looked at her, making the sign of the cross, and took a step out. But then she heard gunshot and retreated back to safety.

Bang! Another shot was heard. "I struck gold!" a voice was heard yelling from outside. "I'm rich!"

Abe yelled to his wife, "Charles and I are going to go see what all the fuss is about. I'm going to switch the sign on the window to 'closed' for now." He looked at Charles with one eyebrow raised. The men cautiously peeked out the door. They could see Crazy Pete, a local frontiersman who didn't come down off the mountain that often. There he was, staggering down the middle of the road too drunk to walk very well. He was holding a jug of spirits in one hand and a bag of so-called gold in the other along with a pistol. He was a big man with a beard that reached down to the middle of his chest. He seemed to smell a little ripe at times but was quite harmless. He hadn't always been that way. He had lost his wife and child in a mountain rock slide a couple of years earlier, and he was never quite the same after that. After the loss of his family he was always seen with a jug of spirits that went with the line of chewing tobacco spittle that ran down the huge bushy beard.

"Ah, it's only Crazy Pete. I wonder if it is real gold this time." Charles's eyes were twinkling at his brother-in-law Abe, and mischief shone in them. Not often were the men seen visiting the saloon in the daytime, as the womenfolk frowned on such behavior. Now would be the perfect opportunity to slip in and out. "I bet Marshal Johnson will be coming out soon. I saw him enter his office when we rode in, but the women don't know that. I could use something to wet my whistle. Are you coming?"

The men quickly walked down to the local saloon. It was only a couple of buildings from the store. If Charles knew that his daughter was going the other way on the street he wouldn't have been very pleased. They opened the swinging doors and entered the saloon, which still smelled of alcohol mixed with cheap perfume from the night before. Samuel, the owner, was behind the bar cleaning glasses. He was the barkeeper too.

"Hi, fellas." Samuel greeted the men with a nod of his head. "I'm surprised to see you in here, especially this early in the afternoon. Is Crazy Pete out there with his bag of gold and jug of spirits? I thought that old coot drank enough for six men last night. You would have thought he would have slept it off by now." He wiped the counter off even though it was as clean as it was going to get. "Didn't know he was packing his pistol though, but I can hear it."

"Yep, that's him out there all right." Abe looked at Charles, and mischief twinkled in his eyes. "We thought this would be the perfect time to come over for a shot of courage without the womenfolk putting up much fuss about it."

Samuel chuckled while placing two shot glasses on the counter top. "What will it be gentlemen?" he asked.

"Whiskey," they both said at the same time.

"It sounds quiet out there. Guess he's had enough." No sooner had the words come out of Samuel's mouth than another shot went off. They all ducked their heads. "Damn that one was close."

The men pick up their shot glasses and slammed them with one gulp. Abe placed a coin on the counter.

They heard the noise spurs made on the wooden walk-ching, ching—and they saw the local marshal go by the saloon door, displaying a tall cowboy hat and spurs on the back of his boots.

"Pete Mundinger, put that gun down," the marshal sternly, looking at the man staggering down the dirt road and creating all the commotion.

Selena had reached Spirit and was on the other side of him; the horse was between her and the armed man. Finally she got him settled down.

Crazy Pete was still waving his gun around in the air as he turned in a circle to show everyone his prize pouch of gold. "Ah, marshal, I'm just having some fun. Look, I struck gold." He hiccupped.

Marshal took a couple more steps—ching, ching, ching; the spurs on his cowboy boots were heard making their way down the steps. He looked to the left and saw the three men with their heads looking over and between the swinging doors of the saloon. The marshal nodded his head in acknowledgment. "Now Pete, I'm a warning ya, put down that gun!" He now was twenty paces from Pete, facing him with his right hand resting over his holstered pistol.

Crazy Pete squinted through bloodshot eyes at the marshal. Was there one of him or two of them? Everything was kind of fuzzy, but he focused on his hand resting on the top of his pistol. With slurred words he replied, "Marshal, I'll lay the gun down, but you can't have my gold." He leaned slowly over to place the gun at his feet and then lost his balance and fell right on his face. The marshal walked over to him; he was lying face first in the dirt road passed out cold. With his foot the marshal kicked the pistol away from Pete, picking up the pouch of gold and looking over at the men who were still watching behind the saloon doors.

"Well, are you going to just stand there gawking or help me get him up?"

Abe and Charles walked out, leaving the doors swinging. Samuel went back to his bar.

That was when Charles noticed his daughter riding on Spirit heading down the road. He yelled at his daughter, "Selena, what are you doing?"

Katie walked out from the corner of the store. "It's okay. She only wanted to get her horse."

Selena turned in a circle. She could feel the heat of her father's gaze glaring at her.

"Pa, I had to get Spirit. I didn't want him to get shot," she weakly replied.

The men were walking toward the passed-out man, but Katie knew that this wasn't going to be good.

"Selena, ride to the stables, and I mean straight there. Get Katie's horse saddled up. We're leaving. If you do not do as I say she is not coming with us." Charles didn't raise his voice much, but his oldest daughter was going to give him gray hair.

"Grab Pete under the arms. We will have to drag him to my office. I have a cot there where he can sleep it off on. As for this gold, it will go in the safe until the old coot can sober up and maybe come to his senses." The marshal directed them, all the while watching Selena do as she was told and thinking to himself that her horse was named after its owner; spirit—that girl sure did have it.

They dragged Pete up the stairs, grunting as they were pulling him the best they could.

"Hey Marshal, you might want him to clean up some. I don't think he has had a bath in a month of Sundays." Both men had handkerchiefs tied around their faces, making sure they covered their noses.

Marshal Johnson chuckled out loud, "Well, at least he has the funds to clean up now." He tossed the bag of gold up into the air, caught it, and continued to follow the men into the jail.

After they had Crazy Pete settled in, they came back out together.

"Charles, I don't know if it's such a good idea to have Katie to stay with you for so long. Selena is so strong-willed. Who knows what mischief they will get into?"

"I shouldn't let her come as punishment, but it is Selena's birthday. I don't want to ruin it with her turning sixteen and all. Abe, if she were a boy I really wouldn't mind as much. She reminds me so much of myself. Let Katie come for a couple of days, and then you and Henrietta come out for dinner."

Running his hand over his head, Charles could tell that Abe was at war with himself. "I guess she can still go." Both men continued toward the store, looking at the women. They had most of the supplies that could be lifted loaded in the wagon. Reid was trying to load up some of the larger items.

The men continued over to get the other supplies ready to go. They still didn't want the wives to find out they had taken a quick trip to the saloon.

"Pa." Selena knew she was pushing her luck but couldn't help but ask. "Can Katie and I still ride ahead of the wagon?"

Charles looked over the sack of flour he was putting in the back of the wagon. Selena was on her horse, and Katie was saddled up and ready to go.

"Did you say good-bye to everyone?" Carolyn asked.

"Yes, Ma, we did." Selena's horse was given her some trouble again, as anxious to go as was the rider. She could tell that Uncle Abe was having second thoughts about Katie coming with them. She liked her uncle, but he could persuade her father at times, and not in her favor.

"Go straight home. You need to get your chores done before you girls even think of leaving the farm." Charles looked at them both, and he meant business too.

Selena replied, trying to hold the laughter out of her eyes, "Okay."

"Bye Mother, bye Father. I will see you in a couple of days or so. I'm sure we will be back if needed." Katie waved at them both. She had a nice dark blue dress on with a wide-rimmed bonnet and her hair tied in a ponytail flowing down her back, Echo, her horse, was chomping at the bit, feeling the excitement of her rider.

The girls left town going slower then they wanted to, but they knew that their parents were watching them. They were still close enough to be called back, and then they would have to follow the wagon. They didn't want to spoil their plans for the day.

Charles had everyone settled in the wagon. With reins in hand it was now time for his family to head home. Abe walked to the side of the wagon and looked at Charles. "Have a safe ride home. Take care of Katie now, you hear?" Good-byes were exchanged, and they were headed on their way.

Selena and Katie rode ahead of the wagon, and their distance started to widen as they got closer to home. Both knew they were supposed to stay in view, but they just couldn't help it. They both wanted to race. Katie's horse was known to be the faster of the two, but Selena was the risk-taker of them. Less than a half mile from home, Selena told Katie, "We're almost home. Race you to the farm?"

Katie replied, "Are you crazy? Your Pa will not be happy."

"Not if he can't catch us. I know you want to. It's only a half mile away. Come on; let's go," Selena challenged.

Grandpa James was tossing hay to the horses in the corral. Grandma Ellen was on the porch darning socks. She spotted her eldest granddaughter first, crouched down and leaning forward against the neck of her horse, her blonde hair mixed in with Spirit's black mane. Not far behind was her other granddaughter, Katie, usually much more prim and proper. Grandma looked at Grandpa, who was closing the gate and walking toward her.

"Well, they don't know we're here, do they?" James told at his wife.

"Ah, no, but they are in for a great big surprise when they come around that corner. They shouldn't be racing those horses like that, and Katie should remember last time she fell off and couldn't walk on her left foot for a week or so."

"Let the girls be girls. Katie has more lives than the old barn cat," Grandpa replied.

Selena had tears running from her eyes as the wind was blowing in them, but she loved a challenge and wasn't going to lose. She looked under her arm; Katie was right on their tail. Both girls noticed the wagon out front at the same time, Grandma and Grandpa had come to visit. They slowed their horses down, but it was too late—they had both been spotted.

"Well, where is the fire, ladies?" Grandpa asked as he walked toward them.

"Grandpa, Grandma, we're so glad to see you," both girls chimed in with big smiles.

Grandpa looked at them both. "You'd better go cool those horses down before your pa gets home. He isn't going to be too happy about you running them so hard. You haven't even been together more than an hour, I would guess, and you are already getting into trouble. But on the other hand, good race, ladies. Katie, you almost had her. A little more road and you would have caught up." Grandpa patted both of the girls' knees as they went by—he loved his grandchildren.

Katie was a little winded, her cheeks rosy red as she rode her horse by the porch trying to straighten her hat. "Hi Grandma."

The girls cooled off their horses by riding them slowly up and down the drive.

"So where are you two going in such a hurry?" Grandma asked.

"We have chores to do, and then we are going to the river swimming," Selena explained.

"Don't worry about it, girls. Grandma has supper cooking. She made birthday cake for Selena's birthday," Grandpa informed them, adding, "Here comes your ma and pa." He pointed to the wagon as it started down the old dirt road. "You both can go to the river. I'll take care of your pa, Selena."

The girls didn't need to be told twice, and they pointed their mounts toward the river, yelling, "Bye."

"So what is the big hurry to go to the river?" Katie asked Selena.

"The Johnson brothers tied a rope from the tree branch that hangs over the rock. You stand on the rock, grab the rope, and swing off it into the water."

"I don't know, Selena. That sounds dangerous." Katie chewed on her bottom lip.

"What do you mean dangerous? You will do just fine."

They reached the river in record time.

Both girls stripped down to their undergarments and entered the flowing water. Living close to the river, they were both taught how to swim at an early age.

Selena climbed on top of the rock first and stood on one leg. While posing she raised her hand above her head and announced proudly, "I'm a river spirit;

watch me fly." Katie giggled slightly while treading water until she snorted water up her nose and started to choke some, but she continued to watch. Selena got out of her pose and grabbed the rope. She stood back, running as fast as she could with the rope in hand, and jumped off the rock. Letting go of the rope she landed in the water with a splash. Selena didn't stay down long but shot up to the top for air, splashing water all around as she came up.

"Wow! That was great. You try it?" Selena climbed back on the rock and tempted Katie, dangling the rope swinging back and forth.

"I don't think so; you know my luck. I might sink like a rock."

"Oh, come on, Katie, you will be fine. I'm right here. What could go wrong?" Selena asked with her hair still dripping water and with a smile of mischief, taunting Katie and splashing water at her.

"Oh, all right," Katie said. "Against my better judgment, Selena Marie Williams." Katie gave in. "Do you remember the last time you said, 'What could go wrong?' It was the bees, and who got stung the most? Me!" Selena was moving through the water toward the rock.

"Oh, never mind about those nasty bees. You're just sweeter than me. That's all that meant. Now just scoot up on the rock." Selena directed her to grab the rope, walk to the back of the rock, and then run like crazy. "But the most important thing is don't forget to let go of the rope after you jump off of the rock." Selena gave the directions while treading water.

Katie chewed on her bottom lip and did as Selena directed. Grabbing the rope she first made a quick sign of the cross and offered a quick prayer. Then she stood back, ran across the rock, jumped off, and landed headfirst in the water in a belly flop and went down into the water. Selena burst out laughing. She thought it was the funniest thing she had ever seen. But why wasn't Katie coming up? The current wasn't running that fast, and Selena had an uneasy feeling developing in the pit of her stomach. She dove down, going into the water and swimming straight. She felt Katie's foot. It was pointing up, and she when pulled on it, it didn't budge. Now what was she going to do? Swimming further down, she opened her eyes. She could see Katie's long hair caught under a log that must have rolled when she went down into the water. Selena's lungs were starting to cry for air. Katie's eyes were huge, with fear shooting from them along with a silent plea of help. Selena could see tiny air bubbles starting to slip from her mouth. Frantically Selena went up for air, screaming as she reached the surface.

Chapter Three

Lone Wolf and Laughing Otter were almost to the river where he had seen his water spirit when he heard the screams. A thought flickered in Lone Wolf's head: she was swimming by herself again; now I will have to protect her from her attackers. Running to the river's edge they could see Selena screaming for help as she still continued to dive under the water, trying to help someone or something. Both guessed that someone was down there who needed help.

The men jumped off their horses before they came to a halt and ran toward the river. Laughing Otter, taking after his namesake, reached Selena first. Selena screamed, pointing down into the water, "Katie is down there. Help her; she's stuck." Laughing Otter dove down. Finding her foot, he reached further down to her leg and looked at her just as the last air exhaled from her mouth. Her eyes were looking right through him, and her hair was just floating in the water. She was motionless as a silent bubble slid from her nose. Seeing that her hair was tangled in an old log stuck to the bottom, he kicked it hard and grabbed her head. Bracing his leg he pushed against the log. Lone Wolf was now on the other side of him, and he moved the log that had rolled onto her long brown hair and had almost imprisoned her in a watery tomb. Rolling the log, they pulled her free. The three came up, and as they broke the surface Katie gasped and coughed for air. Selena was quiet now, and Laughing Otter swam, helping Katie to the bank. Lone Wolf looked at Selena as she swam to the bank ahead of him. She dropped to her knees next to Katie, who was on the river bank still trying to catch her breath.

"Oh my goodness, Katie. Are you okay?" Selena asked.

Coughing and half choking, Katie replied in a raspy whisper, "I'm fine. Just let me get some air, would you?"

She waved her arms, gesturing for Selena to move back and give her some room.

Moving back, Selena noticed that there was a warrior next to Katie and another standing above them. They had saved Katie from drowning, but they now needed to go before they were seen or it would mean trouble for them all. Lone Wolf could see that Katie was going to be okay, but why was Selena looking so frightened? He could see by her expression that she was distressed, or was that a look of disgust on her face?

Selena bolted up, "You need to go now!" She looked at them and pointed toward the woods. She shouted even louder, "Go now. You need to leave." She took her hand as if showing them what she wanted, trying to make them go away. With her palm up, taking her other finger she made a motion like men walking away. Talking even louder she yelled, "Thank you, but you need to go now." She tried to move Lone Wolf toward the woods by pushing on his arm, but he wouldn't budge.

He stood his ground. His bronze arms were now folded over his chest. He looked straight at her and spoke. "I heard you the first time." He raised his voice while surprising her by speaking in perfect English. Shock is the only word Katie could use to describe Selena's face, pure shock. It was funny seeing her friend at a loss for words.

Selena stomped her foot to make her point. "Then why don't you leave?"

Katie sat up with help from Laughing Otter. "Why are you yelling at them to leave? How do you speak our words?" she asked the men.

"We had an old trader living with us a couple of winters ago," Laughing Otter replied.

"I'm trying to save their lives. How does the old saying go: 'Shoot first; ask questions later.' If the Johnson brothers come down here there will be some shooting going on," Selena said.

"She does have a point," Laughing Otter agreed as he helped Katie to her feet. "The Johnson boys are just that—boys; they would not know what they got themselves into." He stuck out his chest just a little more. While speaking, he noticed that Selena had run to where their dresses lay, and with her back turned to them she pulled hers on. He also noticed that his friend was paying way too much attention to this white girl called Selena.

Selena walked over to Katie with her dress in her hand, and as Katie pulled it over her head she helped her put her arms in the sleeves. Katie was not helping much; her arms felt like lead. Selena pulled her closer and wrapped her arms around her with Katie's weight mostly leaning on her.

Looking at them both, she said, "Thank you so much for helping us in our time of need. But for your own safety you should go now." Thinking twice she changed her mind. "Never mind; we will be going now." Dragging the still weak Katie toward the horses and not missing a step she was determined to get them out of here before someone got shot.

Katie tugged back. "Wait. What are your names?" She turned to the men, looking over her shoulder while still being tugged toward the horses.

"Why?" Laughing Otter asked.

"I just would like to thank you for saving my life; a name please?" Katie asked.

Looking at each other, Laughing Otter started to speak, "I am Laughing Otter." He pointed to himself, but before he could finish he was interrupted.

"Lone Wolf," the other man said in a deep voice. "My name is Lone Wolf." His dark brown eyes burned into Selena's soul.

Selena locked her eyes with his, placing a challenge out. She would show him! Her chin came up higher with a flip of her hair, but his look was so deep. It made emotions along with feelings come out that she had never felt before or even known she had. She broke the stare first. With the horses' reins in her hand she walked back to Katie. "I can't thank you both enough, but we have to go now."

Lone Wolf watched Selena grab Katie, who was still much shaken and having trouble getting on the saddle. He watched Selena try to shove her onto it; then she tried to pick her up. The last attempt was to take Katie by her rear end, bending down to lift her up, but the horse kept moving away.

Lone Wolf looked at Laughing Otter and spoke in their native tongue, "We should help her before she gets trampled by her own horse." Laughing Otter chuckled and walked toward the girls. He moved Selena out of the way, as she was now huffing and puffing from effort. He grabbed Katie around the waist and effortlessly lifted her up onto her horse in one fluid motion, leaving Lone Wolf towering over Selena.

She swallowed and looked up at him, saying, "I really could have done that myself, you know! I am not any weakling who needs help."

"So you don't need help? Should I have her put back down and let you try again?" he challenged back.

"No, you have done enough help for the day. We will be going now."

Lone Wolf reached down, grabbed her, and none-too-softly plopped her on her horse. He was so tempted to slap its hind end to see what kind of a rider she was but thought she had had enough excitement for the day.

"Umph" was her only reply.

"Go home, girls. I might not be around next time to help," Lone Wolf told them.

Selena glared at him, thinking to herself how dare he scold her! She was going to be sixteen—a woman; she was not a child.

"Good-bye. Thank you so much," the soft-spoken Katie told them as they started to ride away, waving to them both.

Selena rolled her eyes at her friend, thinking to herself, *Why does she have to be so darn sweet?*

Both men watched as the girls rode away, still standing on the bank of the river. Laughing Otter turned to his friend and said, "Don't even think about it. If you haven't noticed, she is white. She doesn't belong with us."

"I know, but she has such fire, such spirit. She didn't even back down with me towering over her." The men walk to their horses and mounted up.

"She is the one you saw the other day, when you were on your vision quest, wasn't she?" Laughing Otter questioned his friend. "Your father isn't going to tolerate it—you are to be joined with Willow." He was still shaking his head.

The men weren't the only ones who were watching the girls ride off; Scar Face from Chief White Cloud's tribe was at the other side of the river. He wanted his precious Willow for himself, and she shared the same feelings for him. But she was being forced into this arranged marriage with Lone Wolf. Scar Face was thinking up a plan to capture this white woman and make a sacrifice of her. Surely Lone Wolf would come to her rescue, and then he would kill him too. No one would be the wiser, and both would be out of the way. Willow and he would be able to be together as one.

"Are you okay?" Selena asked Katie as they were out of earshot of the two men. "I'm sorry, Katie. I'm so sorry. I didn't know that the logs that were stuck at the bottom would roll. I've jumped off that rock many times. You must have gone down deeper into the water." She glanced over at Katie, her eyes watering.

Katie who had been very quiet was chewing on her bottom lip, a dead giveaway that she was either worried or thinking about something. "He likes you, you know." She glanced at Selena.

Selena looked at her, all innocent. "Who likes me?"

"Don't play dumb with me, Selena. You know who I mean—the taller of the two, Lone Wolf; he likes you."

"Well, I don't like him," she answered back.

"I think thou protest too much, my friend," Katie teased.

"Seriously, aren't you at all shook up about what happened today? I know Grandpa said you have as many lives as an old barn cat, but you have to admit you have used a few." It was Selena who now chewed on her bottom lip.

Katie thought quietly before she answered. Selena was looking down and counting the black-eyed daisies along the trail as they rode by. "I have said this before: my journey here is going to be short, Selena. I need to make the most of everything."

Selena turned to Katie. "Don't say that. You have always said that, and I don't understand how or why you want to leave us." A look of hurt came over Selena's face. "What Grandma's tea leaves say isn't always true; you know that. Your father would be very upset if he heard you speak that way."

"Let's just drop it, okay? We are almost back to the farm." Katie turned her head, looking right at Selena. "Let's not say a word to anyone. This is our secret, Selena."

The girls stopped their horses before they turned to the bend in the rode that would take them into eyesight of the farm.

They knew this would require the secret handshake. Selena rode around to the front of Katie so that they were now facing each other.

They both began to chant: "Friends are friends, that are we, never to tell of what we see, to the grave we will take, spit in your hand, the secret friendship shake." They chanted the verses twice, spit in their hands, and shook on it. No one knew about it. Well, there had only been the one time when Katie's mom caught them and made them wash the spit off their hands instantly with soap. *But this was better than slicing the skin on each hand and placing them together as Selena wanted to do when we were eight to mix blood for the secret handshake,* Katie thought to herself with a smile on her face.

Both girls smiled as they rode down the road to the farm. Grandma was ringing the big black bell that would let the men know that it was time to come in from the field. Supper was on the table.

"Hello girls. Ready for supper?" she asked them.

"Yes," they replied.

Charles looked at both girls as they sat down. He was suspicious. What had happened today? They were trying very to hide something.

"So how was your swim?" he asked.

Both replied, "Fine."

Taking a biscuit, he slowly buttered it while looking at them, suspicious. "I talked to the Johnson boys this afternoon. They said they saw two warriors from a neighboring tribe riding upriver from where you two were. You didn't run into any trouble today, did you?" he asked.

Katie took that moment to choke on her milk while spilling the rest all over the table. Selena knew that she had to think fast. "No, Pa. We didn't see anyone. We just swam at the river for a while." Changing the subject, she added, "Can we eat cake and open gifts now?"

Coming to the girls' rescue, Carolyn said, "I think that would be a great idea."

The first gift opened was from Katie. It was the peacock-feathered hat that matched her eyes. A new apron was from her parents. From her brother and sister she got a bouquet of wild flowers. Grandma and Grandpa handed down the family Bible.

Chapter Four

A different kind of wind was felt as Lone Wolf got back to the village. He could see that Chief White Cloud was already in the ceremony lodge meeting with his father along with the other leaders. He was greeted by his mother, who promptly told him that he had been summoned to the lodge. As he entered the lodge, he noticed that his father and the others were already seated around a small fire, passing the ceremonial peace pipe. As was the custom he entered the circle to the left and offered acknowledgment to the four directions of the wind. He located his seat and sat down. All eyes were on him as he took a big puff of the ceremonial pipe.

"My son, have you forgotten our meeting?" his father asked.

He nodded in acknowledgment. "It will not happen again."

Chief White Cloud looked around, carefully choosing his words before speaking. "Many seasons we have been two tribes sharing the bountiful land." He looked around at the nodding heads. "The white eyes are coming into our land more and more each day." He spoke clearly and slowly. "So far there have been not many conflicts, but I feel that soon that day will change. If we have our tribes unite together as one, we will be stronger and more powerful and the white eyes will not bother us. That is why I came today along with my daughter, to join her together with Lone Wolf in marriage."

Two Timbers looked at his son and saw that his face was not showing any emotion, but his eyes were speaking loudly. He spoke his words carefully as he replied to Chief White Cloud. "Our tribes joining together would be a strong force to contend with. Willow is a beautiful young princess who will make a good wife for my son, Lone Wolf." Lone Wolf didn't realize that he was holding his breath until his father finished speaking, and then he let it out slowly. He knew that it was going to happen whether he agreed to it or not, but that was before he ran into his green-eyed water spirit. The pipe was handed back to him. He inhaled a breath, but it wasn't as big as it should have been.

"Then it is settled." White Cloud rejoiced. "The joining of our tribes will take place in three weeks, when the moon is at its fullest."

"Three weeks it will be." Two Timbers nodded his head in agreement as he spoke the words.

All left the ceremonial tipi. Most went to the community fire, where they would be food passed around while dancers swayed to the beating drums. Lone Wolf was looking for Laughing Otter, not really paying any attention to where he was going, when he collided right into Willow.

His foot came down hard on her big toe. Willow let out a yelp. She pulled her leg in tight and caressed her toe. "Watch it," she said. She glanced up, and a look of surprise overtook her. She blushed and then quickly looked away.

"I'm sorry," Lone Wolf said. "I wasn't looking." He knelt down beside her and reached out a hand to check her toe.

She pulled her foot back. "It's okay," she replied. "Are you hungry? I could get you something to eat," she asked as she continued to walk with him toward the fire.

He slowed his stride so she could match his more easily. They sat down by the fire and were passed corn cakes with honey to dip in. He finished his in a couple bites. He looked at Willow. She had beautiful raven-black hair that was parted down the middle and braided on both sides. She had large almond-shaped eyes with the irises so dark that it was hard to see where the pupil started and ended. As Willow nibbled on her corn cake she felt more than saw Lone Wolf watching her, and she smiled with her white teeth showing in the fire light. She tilted her head to the left. "What is it?" Her voice was seductive.

With a slight grin, he replied, "You have honey dribbled on your chin." He slowly placed his thumb on her face and wiped the honey off, thinking to himself that he had grown up with Willow as a child but thought of her more as a sister then a wife. Looking up at the stars he remembered his vision. He would just have to leave it in the Great Spirit's hands.

She blushed and moved back a little as his hand slipped back to his side. "Thank you." Her heart fluttered a little until she saw Scar Face glaring at her from the other side.

Scar Face glared at them he was sitting with the other warriors from White Cloud's tribe. He was the one who wanted to marry Willow. He was the one who had won her heart until this arranged marriage was brought about. He tore off his meat off the bone with a jerk of his head, wiping the grease on his legs. He chewed loudly but still continued to glare at them both. Lone Wolf must have his Willow under a spell. Why else would she be fluttering her eyelashes at him? She had sworn her true love to Scar Face. He watched Lone Wolf excuse himself from Willow to join the men chanting and dancing to the haunting sound of the drums. Willow's eyes were following him until she felt Scar Face looking intensely at her; from the other side she lowered her eyes.

Chapter Five

Katie and Selena were up in the loft together. Amy was sleeping in Reid's bed, as he had gone to their grandparents' house to stay, thinking that there would be too much girly stuff with Katie there. With too many girls around he felt outnumbered. Also, his grandfather was teaching him how to whittle. He had even given him his own pocket knife, which Reid was ever so proud of.

"Selena, if you take your hat off, I will brush your hair for you. The unusual feathers on your hat match the color of your eyes," Katie said.

"Yes, they are just like me," she teased as she pranced around the room with her new hat on, strutting around like a chicken. "What a strange day it has been." Her step slowed down as she remembered the river, all that water, and Katie not coming up. She looked at Katie, who was sitting on her bed. Her eyes teared up; she couldn't help it.

"I'm sorry. It was my fault," Selena said. "I shouldn't have talked you into it."

Katie shook her head. "Forget it. I mean, what happened to me. Not the rest of it."

"Rest of what?" Selena asked.

"You know."

Selena shook her head.

Katie clasped her hands to her chest. "Oh, Lone Wolf, you're so handsome and rugged."

Selena felt the heat rush to her face. She swiped at Katie, who simply danced away. Katie snatched Selena's new hat from the table and put it on. "Do you like my new hat, Mr. Wolf?" She then pulled the hat off and batted her eyelashes. "Or did you prefer me in nothing at all?"

Selena gasped. "Katie!"

Katie just puckered her lips and gave Selena a crooked smile.

"You girls keep it down up there," Charles called from below.

Selena snatched up her pillow and swatted Katie. Katie began to topple but managed to reach out a hand and grab Selena's arm before she fell. The two collapsed in a heap on the bed, giggling.

Jumping up, Selena went to sit in the chair by the window. Katie could still sit on the bed and brush her hair there. Katie and Selena were both lost in their own thoughts. Katie couldn't believe her luck today. Selena couldn't stop thinking about Lone Wolf—the dark face, the high cheekbones, the brown eyes that looked right through her. He had muscular arms and a solid chest, and she felt her face getting red again and her heart beating a little faster than her liking. Katie was in mid-stroke when she noticed that her friend's scalp was turning red.

"Selena, am I brushing too hard?" she asked. "Your scalp is turning pink."

"Ah, no." Changing the subject, she was remembering how it felt in Lone Wolf's arms, "Ma wants us to pick raspberries tomorrow. Do you feel up to berry picking? With your luck you will step on a snake or a bee's nest. Ouch!" Katie pulled Selena's hair, handing her the brush while beating her to the other side of the bed.

"Nice—you call yourself a friend? I wouldn't know what to expect if you said you were my enemy," Katie teased her back. She was now under the blankets where Amy shared their bed and was fluffing her pillow. She had on her nightgown, and her hair in one long braid came over her shoulder. She had her nightcap on, but she still got chilly in the night air. Selena braided her hair, climbed in, and put her cold toes on Katie's legs.

"That was cold; you are such a brat," Katie said.

Selena giggled at how many times Katie had slept over when they were growing up.

"Good night, Katie."

"Good night. Say your prayers."

"Oh, I almost forgot. I will say an extra one for you."

"Why?"

"'Cause you have all sorts of luck, but that was bad luck today, Katie, bad luck," she said softly.

Both girls lay all tucked in with the blankets up to their chins. They had their eyes closed and their hands folded on their chests in prayer.

Katie opened her eyes. Selena was notorious for snoring, and it took her all of twenty seconds of prayer before she nodded off to sleep. Katie looked out the window, trying to go to sleep but needing to finish her prayers. *Dear Lord, please bless my family and my friends and keep them all safe. Please help those who are in need or less fortunate, Lord. Thank you for the two brave souls who helped me get untangled from the logs under the water. I know you gave me this beautiful long hair, but it was almost the death of me.* Her eyes were closed so tight that the tears were sliding out. *I feel in my heart a heaviness and sadness. I love being here but know that my time is short. I sense it, and I have always known it would be that way. Please grant me the strength to endure what you wish will be for me.* Katie drifted off to sleep with Selena softly snoring next to her. It felt like she had just dozed off when Aunt Carolyn was calling their names.

"Girls, time to get up. Amy is collecting eggs, and Pa is feeding the animals. Come help me make breakfast."

"Yes, Ma. We're on our way." Both girls climbed out of bed and washed up with the pitcher of water. They pulled on new dresses in record time and brushed and braided their hair for each other, and down the ladder they both came.

It was the usual breakfast: eggs, fried potatoes from last night's supper, and bacon. Katie's tummy rumbled as they were setting the table together. They looked at each other and giggled. All sat down to eat. As Pa said grace all was quiet.

Soon Katie thought she was going to explode if she had one more bite, but the biscuits were so yummy, she put a couple in her pocket for later.

Charles looked at Carolyn. His curly brown hair had been brushed but was now windblown from being outside. A few lines showed by his eyes when he smiled, highlighting his dimples. They were his best feature, along with his skin tanned from the sun. "Today I'm going to work in the back pasture. I will be close to the house if you need anything." He looked at Amy, who had freckles on her nose and cheeks. "What are your plans today, young lady?" Charles asked.

"I'm helping Ma with the quilt we are making for my bed." Smiling from ear to ear she stuck her tongue out at Selena as if to say, "Ha you don't get to help us."

Selena jumped into the conversation. "We're going berry picking for the pies we're going to have at dinner tonight."

Amy replied as any sister would before their mother could answer, "Good luck, Katie. Hope you like picking berries. Selena eats more then she picks. Ouch!" she cried out as Selena kicked her under the table.

"Girls, that will be enough." Carolyn looked at both of them, giving them the motherly look. Turning toward Katie, she said, "Are you sure you want to stay with us? How can you handle this sisterly love?" She smiled as she sipped the last of her morning tea.

Katie winked back, "Oh, I'm an only child, remember. Grandma said staying here would give me character."

Charles laughed out loud, and so did everyone else around the table. Getting up, he adjusted his suspenders over his shoulder and reached for his old worn-out hat that kept the sun out of his eyes. Opening the door he saw that the morning was just breaking. "Have a good day, ladies, in whatever adventures you may find yourself in today. But any sign of trouble I want you both back home here, you hear?" He looked at Katie. "Try to keep Selena from getting herself or you into trouble. Watch out for that old black bear that has been hanging around that berry patch and also any other two-legged man or beast."

"Bye, Pa," the girls chimed together.

"Ma, are the buckets in the barn?" Selena asked.

"Yes. Why are you wearing your new hat? You should keep it as your good hat," Carolyn told her.

Selena replied as she walked toward the door, "It's just berry picking."

Katie rolled her eyes. "I told her the same thing. That's a Sunday morning church hat, not a berry-picking hat. Who is she trying to impress, the old black bear?"

"Ma, it will keep the sun out of my eyes," she pleaded. "I just love it, and I promise to be extra careful."

"Don't get it dirty or lose it either, and no berry stains—they won't come out," she gently scolded Selena.

Selena turned and took a few steps and gave her a great big hug with a peck on her cheek. "Okay, I promise to be very careful, Ma."

"The hat sure does make your eyes stand out. They look more like a jade color than green. My, just look at you. Sixteen years old, a young woman." Her mom's eyes were teary looking at her daughter, but she was right—her womanly figure was all there and then some.

The girls went to the barn to get their berry-picking buckets, saddled up their horses, grabbed their lunches, and waved good-bye.

"Be careful of that old bear, snakes, and beehives, girls." Carolyn was standing just outside the door wiping her hands on her white apron, and Amy was next to her, waving good-bye.

"Bye," both girls replied at the same time.

Just out of eyesight and earshot they were on for the race to the berry patch. It was almost as if their horses knew, it because they were chomping at the bit to have their own heads. Just out of sight, mischief was in both of the girls' eyes. They rode side by side, and with a common nod the race was on. Both girls kicked their horses into a faster pace. Katie was in the lead this time, but Selena was right behind. If she leaned a little closer she could have touched the tail of Katie's horse.

Chapter Six

Scar Face and his band of close warrior friends had been taking turns watching the farm and waiting for the girls to leave by themselves.

His temper was quick. He should have picked off the family one by one, but better judgment had won over his emotions. He also didn't want the satisfaction of a fast death for this white girl; a slow tortured painful one was what he had planned. He would lead Lone Wolf to them so he could watch as the precious life slipped from this white face. For all the years of pain he had inflicted on him, payback was what he wanted the most.

Scar Face remembered the way he had seen Lone Wolf look at the white girl when he happened upon them by the river. He should be happy that Lone Wolf was interested in someone else other than his Willow. But how could he turn his eyes toward another woman when he had the honor of being joined in less than a month with Willow? Was she also not good enough for him? Had he heard that Scar Face wanted her for himself and deemed her not worthy?

Even when they were younger, Lone Wolf always seemed to be one step ahead of him. They were not of the same tribe, but a competition between the two had broken out at an early age. Lone Wolf had been the first to slay a bear, a great honor as they entered into manhood. Also, at the tribal gathering when neighboring tribes came to gather to see who was the strongest, fastest, and the most skilled warrior, Scar Face always seemed to come in second.

There was one thing that Lone Wolf had that Scar Face did not. One day when his father passed on or was unable to continue his duties, he would be chief. Scar Face knew that if he were to marry Willow then he would also be a chief. Lone Wolf hadn't shown any feelings toward Willow, so why should he have her? Scar Face had wooed her over many months, until she finally professed her love to him. He had gathered enough horses now that he could offer them to her father, Chief White Cloud, so he could ask for his daughter's hand in marriage. Then one day he too would be chief, finally an equal to Lone Wolf. Then he would declare war on Lone Wolf and his tribe, and when he won he would reign over them all; he would be so powerful then.

He clenched his teeth in anger, remembering the way Lone Wolf had also looked at Willow when they were at the ceremony that last night. Well, he couldn't have them both. He had been so furious with her father when he found out that he had announced his plan to join the two tribes as one, even when Scar Face was going to ask for her hand in marriage. His plan would have to work.

Well, he was going to make them all pay. He was going to have that blonde girl along with an added bonus—her pretty friend too-quite soon. He might change his mind and let them live as his slaves and then kill Lone Wolf instead. He smiled an evil smile, thinking of all the fun he was going to have—he just couldn't wait.

Just then he saw the older man leaving the cabin to make his way to the field, a usual day for him.

Seeing the older woman go inside he considered that it would be easy to torch the house and barn. He had accomplished the same thing just the other day; these white men were so trusting. Looking at his friends eagerly waiting for his signal, he decided to leave the rest of the family for another day—he wanted that blonde girl. Silently they all faded back into the woods to their horses to follow the two unsuspecting girls on horseback.

Katie slowed down. Selena was going to pass her but slowed to a trot alongside her. "What's up?" she asked.

"It's such a lovely day, and we're almost there—let's go slower. I wouldn't want to run into that bear that hangs around or to run it over if it happens to be in the raspberry bush."

"Pa was just kidding. We haven't seen that old bear for years now."

"Better to not take a chance, don't you think?" Katie looked at her.

Selena thought that Katie had the eyes of an old soul. She was always the more cautious of the two.

"Oh, I can see the berries from here." Salina's stomach growled.

"Was that your stomach or the old bear?" Katie giggled.

Selena just rolled her eyes. "Funny!" She stuck out her tongue, always one to be a rogue, and nudged her horse into a trot. "Ha, beat you. I was first here." She slid off her horse, removed the saddle, and staked her out to nibble on the grass.

"Only by a horse's length, cheater. Let's get to berry picking. It shouldn't take that long to get done. They are very big this season. What do you want to do when we are done?" Katie asked.

Peeking from beneath her hat, Selena answered, "I guess the river would be out of the question."

"How could you even think of going back to the river after what happened yesterday!" Katie exclaimed.

"Yeah, guess you're right. There isn't any sign of bear; haven't seen a snake either. All is good," Selena answered, changing the subject.

Lone Wolf was up early that morning. His wolf pup was walking beside him, waiting for him to drop a tasty piece of jerky. Now where was Laughing Otter? He was to meet him early that morning. He walked to just a few feet from his friend's tipi and watched him step out, stretch, and rub the sleep out of his eyes. Shaking his head to himself he thought that it looked like Laughing Otter had enjoyed the festival last night just a little too much.

Laughing Otter spied his friend and stood up a little straighter, as if all was well and he wasn't feeling the effects of last night's celebration. But his shoulders drooped a little when he noticed Lone Wolf grinning with one corner of his lip turned up slightly more like a smirk.

"Not a word, my friend. It is too early in the morning for that," he grumbled.

"I wasn't going to say anything. What kind of friend would I be if I did?" Lone Wolf replied.

The men continued to get their horses. They were going to hunt bear today.

Wanting to change the subject, Laughing Otter broke the silence. "I saw you sitting by Willow last night."

"So I can't sit and talk to a friend?" Lone Wolf replied defensively.

"Well, I'm a little confused. The last time I talked to you, you were so sure your soul mate was that white girl; you know, your Green Eyes? I know you thought it would be a good match, but I'm glad you seem to have come to your senses. Have you forgotten that her people don't like our people?" Laughing Otter just couldn't help himself.

"It isn't over yet. Remember that I have a duty to uphold. One day, when my father passes on to the spirit world, I will be chief. I will do what is expected but I will also follow my heart."

"Right. Good luck with that. You're going to have to do the same as your father did, and his father's father did. It's our way," Laughing Otter replied.

"The elders will listen to my vision. It has to mean something. I would not have felt it so strongly if things were not to be played out differently. Only time will tell," Lone Wolf said.

"Did you see Scar Face the other night? He was not very happy that you were talking and sitting by Willow. I heard that he wanted to be with Willow and that she had feelings for him," Laughing Otter said.

"I'm not that concerned about him and Willow. What I am the most concerned about is that if I find out he is the one causing all the trouble with the white people he is going to have to worry about me. That last homestead where the family was killed and everything was torched was not that far away. The white folks are pointing at our tribe and not his.

"You really think he had something to do with that?" Laughing Otter asked.

"Yes I do. It has Scar Face written all over it," he answered.

Both were lost in their own thoughts as they continued to ride.

Chapter Seven

Katie stood up, stretching her back, which had started to cramp from being bent over for so long reaching for berries. She stood up and looked over the berry patch but didn't see Selena. "Selena, where are you?"

Selena had been kneeling on the ground but looked up. Katie could see the top of her hat as she mumbled with her mouth full, "Over here."

"You're not eating all the berries, are you?"

"No!" The reply was a little quick. She looked in her pail—only about a fourth full-thinking to herself, *I thought I had put more in it.* She stood up.

As Katie looked back at Selena she couldn't hold back the laughter. Holding her stomach she was bent over laughing.

Selena looked up at here in bewilderment. "What are you laughing at?"

"Your dress has a rip in the shoulder, and your hat is all crooked, which your Ma isn't going to be happy with, especially if you lose it or get dirt on it. My bucket is almost full; just how many berries have you picked?"

"Well, first I tripped on a log and spilled some of my berries. I have about this much." They both looked inside of her pail.

With a smile on her face, Katie said, "So you mean to say you lost most of your berries."

"Yep."

"So how come you have berry stains on both sides of your mouth and a seed stuck in your front tooth?"

Selena instantly brought her hands up to her mouth, trying to rub the stains she must have gotten from the juicy berries, but from the look she was getting from Katie it wasn't working.

"I only had a couple. I just wanted to make sure they were sweet."

"You are so funny." Katie grabbed one of the raspberries off the bush and popped it into her mouth. "It looks like you ate a couple dozen with the evidence being an empty bucket and a seed stuck in your front tooth." She ducked as Selena chucked a berry at her. With a small giggle she set her bucket down and tossed one back, hitting Selena right in the head. The woods suddenly went silent; something felt wrong. That is when the girls noticed that they weren't alone. Selena was just about to give in on the berry fight when she turned to Katie only to see a native standing not two feet from her. The rest of the warriors all stood up out of the bushes; they were surrounded.

"Katie, come by me." Katie walked over to Selena.

The circle of warriors were closing in, and the girls stood back to back turning in a circle not wanting to have their back to any of them. But there were three or four of the natives, and they were just two girls. The men weren't smiling either, and none looked like Lone Wolf or Laughing Otter. Katie grabbed Selena's hand, thinking to herself, *Now what? Can't we just have one normal day together without mishap?*

"Do you want our berries?" Katie asked. *God, she was so naïve,* Selena thought. She shot Katie a look that told her to be quiet. "We are just leaving. You can have the whole place to yourself." Selena elbowed her in the ribs to try to make her stop talking. They weren't here for the damn berries! The warrior with a scar on his face was now only inches from Selena. He lifted his hand, and yanking her hat off, he threw it in the bushes. Her blond hair had been tucked up in it but came crashing down in waves on her shoulders all the way down her back. He stretched his hand, took a curl, and rubbed it between his thumb and finger. Then he wrapped it around his finger and gently tugged it, thinking to himself, *So soft.* Selena didn't even dare breathe—what was he doing? She could see the different emotions play across his face: softness, envy, and then anger, and she couldn't help but try pulling away. Well, she wasn't going to just sit here like a lamb being led into slaughter.

"What are you doing? Give me my hat back," Selena yelled at him and pulled back. He released her hair, and she tried to walk to where her hat was. But Scar Face was not used to being spoken to by any woman, let alone a paleface. As punishment his hand came up quickly to slap her across the face. Her head swung to the side from the force of it. She stumbled back into Katie, her ears ringing from the blow. Tears welled up, threatening to overflow onto her cheeks, which were red along with her lip. It was split from her teeth, and she could taste blood in her mouth.

Katie helped support her friend, and she whispered to her, "Are you okay? What do they want? That mean man looked like he wanted to kill you. I hope this wasn't their berry patch." Selena had tears coming out of the corner of her eyes. She would not give them the satisfaction of seeing her cry, but God, the side of her face was just throbbing.

Scar Face walked up to her and raised his hand, threatening her again. She was trembling inside but stood her ground. "You stay here. Do not move." He spoke in broken English. Both girls nodded their heads in agreement. In his native tongue he barked orders to his fellow warriors. The girls watched them get their horses. They were speaking in their own language, and neither knew what they were saying.

Katie asked in a whispered voice, "Are you okay?"

"I will be fine; they have our horses—let's hope that's all they want."

"Do you think they are from the same tribe as Lone Wolf or Laughing Otter?"

"It couldn't hurt if we told them their names. Maybe they are from the same tribe."

Their conversation was cut short when the man with the scar, who must be the leader, came back. "Come with us." Not a question but a demand. Both girls were grabbed by the arms, and a gag was stuffed in their mouths, making it impossible to swallow and even harder to breath. Selena's lips were so numb it didn't hurt yet, but she knew this wasn't looking good.

The warriors tied their hands in front of them. Selena could feel the rope bite into her wrists. Then several rough hands grabbed her and tossed her onto Spirit. Both girls' eyes were as wide as they could be; here they were surrounded by Indians riding away to who knew where.

They rode for hours until they came to a small creek that fed off the larger river. Scar Face with his band of warriors all dismounted to get water from the creek to drink; even the horses were thirsty. Selena tried to talk, but all she could manage was mumbled words behind her gagged mouth. Her mouth was so dry, and the water trickling from the creek made her try to swallow. She just wanted a drink of water. She watched the leader as he said something to his men, who came over only to drag each girl off their horse. When their feet touched the ground they both went down, their legs sore from sitting in one position for so long. At least they had taken the gags out, but they didn't untie their hands.

Selena whispered to Katie, "Crawl if you can to the creek. We need water." Katie slowly turned to just stare at her, her eyes glazed above her tear-streaked cheeks. She was in shock.

"Katie, move it!" Selena helped her crawl a little way until they were almost to the edge of the creek. She got to her feet and helped Katie up until they both dropped to their knees and drank the sweet flowing water. Oh, the water was so good. They could feel they were being watched as the men just waited for the girls to make a foolish mistake. Katie's stomach growled, and she looked at Selena.

"You should have eaten more berries; then you wouldn't be that hungry." Selena tried to lighten the mood.

Katie couldn't help but smile while shaking her head. "Yeah, I had a biscuit in my pocket from breakfast, if it is not all crumbs by now. Well, at least we didn't get attacked by the bear." She looked at Selena, who was crouching down in the water with her dress pulled up.

"What are you doing?" Katie asked.

"I have to use the bathroom. Better to have a wet dress from water than a smelly one from pee," Selena replied.

Katie stared in disbelief, "I'm not dropping my underdrawers in front of that wild bunch."

Selena was cupping her hands and trying to put the cool water on her bruised lip and cheek. Still knee deep in the water she looked at Katie. "Don't be such a prude; if you don't go now so be it."

With slumped shoulders Katie decided to join Selena.

Selena saw the leader barking orders once again to his men, and the girls knew that it was time leave. They trudged up the small bank back to their horses and ceremoniously were dumped onto their backs.

"Where do you think they are taking us?" Selena asked.

"Shhh. They didn't put the gag back in." Katie glared at her.

"Well, I don't know what they have planned, but I don't like it at all."

Selena looked around. How was she going to get them out of this one?

Katie turned in her saddle. "Don't even think about it. We are not good enough to try to run away."

"Pa will know what to do. We should have been back by now. I bet they have already been to the berry patch and are on our trail right now," Selena told her.

Chapter Eight

Lone Wolf and Laughing Otter were hunting the same bear that had been hanging by the woods around the berry patch. Lone Wolf knelt on the ground looking at a set of bear tracks.

"It's not the old bear, but it is a big one. The meat will help us through the winter, and the fur will keep me warm." Lone Wolf was ever so serious.

"I think you will need a little honey by your side to help you stay warm this winter. Will she be blonde or dark-haired, or maybe both?" Laughing Otter couldn't resist teasing his friend.

"Let's not go there again this morning," Lone Wolf warned.

"Well, I know you don't want to be reminded of all of this." He was pointing at the berry patch. "What do you think took place in there?"

Lone Wolf looked up. He could see that the berry patch was in shambles. Lone Wolf walked toward the middle with Laughing Otter right next to him. They spotted the buckets of half-picked berries lying on the ground. Laughing Otter spotted the hat. Lone Wolf had seen the likes of those feathers on the hat in his vision. Upon further inspection he could see blonde hair stuck in it.

"Look at this imprint. It is the white woman's shoe print, the same as at the creek the other day," Laughing Otter pointed out. He looked up at his friend. "Selena and Katie."

"Now what kind of mischief are they getting themselves into again? Doesn't that look like the mark of White Cloud's horses?" They looked at the mark of a hoof print that was left in the sand. "That definitely is from a shoed horse—Selena and Katie's horse."

"What does White Cloud want with the two girls? It looks like they were forced to go with them. Look at how they were dragged to their horses."

"This has Scar Face written all over it. He wasn't that friendly the other night. I knew he liked Willow. They had been kind of a couple until her father decided to join us together—you know, the one tribe thing. But what does it have to do with the two girls?" he wondered out loud.

The men mounted their horses and started to search for the girls' tracks. The sun would be going down in a couple of hours, and they would make faster time than Scar Face could without the girls to hinder them.

After searching the area they came across the covered tracks. It would be easy to follow them now.

Lone Wolf knew how cruel Scare Face could be. He had been captured as a young boy by an enemy tribe, which is how he got the scar that came down through his left eyebrow and left cheek and part of his upper lip down to his chin. He had been beaten daily and made a slave for two and a half years, all at the tender age of five. He had to learn to fend for himself by grabbing scraps from the dogs to eat. He had to learn at an early age how to survive. He was found by Chief White Cloud after a battle in the village he was in. The chief took pity on him, and he was taken and given to one of the younger couples who couldn't have children. But Scar Face could never get over the cruelty brought upon him while he was in captivity. It now seemed that he would live a life of hatred when things didn't go his way.

Chapter Nine

S elena knew that they had ridden up the mountain and were halfway down the other side. Her backside felt every move her horse made. She was a good rider, but she had never ridden this long. She looked at Katie, who seemed to be faring the same as her. She was not the stronger of the two, but she was holding her own. Selena could hear the horses' hooves crunching the pine needles as they stepped through the woods. Selena thought to herself that it had been a dry season this year and a little bit of lightning and this forest would go up in smoke—it was very dry. Thinking of smoke, she thought she could smell some. Lifting her head up, which had been resting chin on chest, Selena could see that a small fire had been started with a bigger pile of logs stacked a couple feet away from it.

Looking in Katie's direction, she said, "Do you see the fire?"

"Yes, but what are they going to do with us?" Katie whimpered.

"Don't worry about the fires. They are not for us," Selena tried to reassure her.

As they road into the camp they were greeted with a war cry that sent shivers down both the girls' spines. Their horses came to a halt. The girls knew to move their legs a little to try bring the circulation back into them before they were made to dismount. But they were not fast enough. Katie was grabbed first by the tall warrior who smelled of bear grease. He pulled her off her horse and stared at her with hatred. She couldn't help it—the smell was so overpowering that she wrinkled her nose. "Yuck," was all Katie could think, but she didn't realize she had spoken it out loud. The warrior didn't know what she said, but the look on her face told him she wasn't impressed. He jerked her by the back of the head and twisted her head back until she screamed with pain. She struggled, kicking and scratching at him, and tried to push against his chest. But he was too strong. He yanked out his knife and raised it high into the air. Selena screamed loudly and tried to run to Katie but was held back. Katie's eyes were wild with fright as the knife descended down, and she closed her eyes, unable to watch. She was sure this was the last moment of her life. "Lord, I love you all so very much. Please watch over my ma and pa." Swoosh, the knife came down, swiping across her hair to cut it just below her ears. Victory was his. He held his hand up high in the air, yelling a victory cry while showing everyone his newly acquired prize. Katie was dragged to a tree and shoved on the ground, her arms tied behind her. Selena joined her none too ceremoniously. Her back was scraped by the tree bark, and her arms felt like they were being pulled from their sockets. Katie was defeated and just sat there with her head hung, crying silently.

"Katie, are you okay?" Selena whispered.

Katie continued crying. She was tired and just wanted to go home. She didn't want to be there.

Katie looked at Selena. Her big brown eyes looked huge. With her hair so short her cheekbones stood out and her almond-shaped eyes were very pronounced.

Stuttering, Katie replied, "I didn't say anything bad. I promise I really didn't say anything bad. Why did he do that?" Katie was shaking uncontrollably. Her teeth were chattering, and she could feel the cool breeze blowing on the back of her neck where her long hair used to be.

"It's okay. Help will be here soon. I know our folks must be worried. It is almost dark, and we should have been back home by now. Katie, we will be found, or we will get out of this. Look at me!" Katie just stared at Selena. "I'm going to get us out of here one way or another, I promise, and you know I will not make a promise that I can't keep," Selena told her.

"I know you keep your promises, but Selena, we are in over our heads with this one. I just don't want to get hurt anymore or die trying to get away." Her spirit had been broken.

"We are not going to die; we will get out of this," Selena reassured her.

Selena watched as the warriors placed even more wood over the fire. She could see that they were drinking firewater like the jug Crazy Pete had been drinking out of, and they were now dancing around the smaller fire chanting and carrying on. Why were there two stakes in the ground by the front of the larger fire pit? Selena didn't like that at all. She was getting a worried feeling in the pit of her stomach.

"Hey, do you see a woman over there?" Selena asked Katie through her cracked lip. Her face hurt from being slapped earlier. She hadn't realized it until they stopped riding; then the throbbing started.

43

"Yes, she is talking to the one with the scar on his face," Katie mumbled. "Maybe she came to help us?"

"She doesn't look too happy with him, does she? It looks like they are having words. How come she keeps pointing at us? It looks like he is grabbing her arm and forcing her to come over here," Selena told her.

"Is he going to tie her to the tree too? Maybe he captured her as well," Katie said.

"I don't know, but look at her. She is trying to act brave, but she looks scared and not that happy with what is going on," Selena replied.

"If they come over maybe we could distract them or pretend to get sick—make yourself throw up. Maybe she will have sympathy on us and we can get away. Katie, are you listening to me or not?" Selena asked. Her reply was silence.

Chapter Ten

S car Face had promised he wouldn't touch the firewater because last time he did he almost lost Willow's love. But he was so happy that he had captured the two white girls that he had his share to drink that night. He tricked Willow to come there so he could show his love to her by the sacrifice he would make. She didn't know that if he couldn't have her, Lone Wolf would not have her or the blonde one either.

Looking up, Scar Face could see his Willow riding to him, and he smiled his greeting to her: "You made it."

Willow was taking everything in that she could see, from the fire to the stakes in front of them, "What is all of this, Scar Face?" she asked.

Walking up to her he helped her down. "Come with me, my Princess Willow. I will show you what I have done for you," he said, using her titled name.

Willow continued to look around until she spotted the two girls, who were tied up and not looking in the best of shape.

"Why are their two white girls here, Scar Face?" she asked.

Looking right into her eyes while taking her hand, he spoke, "I brought them here as a sacrifice for you, to show my love. You do not have to join with Lone Wolf. The two tribes can join together without marriage," he replied.

Willow looked surprised as a knot of fear was starting to build in her stomach. "This will bring awful trouble to our tribe, especially with the white men. They have been on edge since the last time there was an incident. You need to release the girls." She softened her tone, trying another approach. "If you love me you will bring them back to where you found them now or just let them go." She slowly removed her hand from his.

Looking irritated with her, he replied, "Why would I do something like that? No one will know it was I who did this. I want them to blame Two Timber's tribe and Lone Wolf," he sneered.

Willow could tell that Scar Face had been drinking; he was past reasoning with. This was a side that she had only seen once before. She should have known better than to come out here to meet with him alone. Now how was she going to fix this?

She looked at the two girls. Fear was written all over their faces, and she could tell by their beseeching looks that they wanted her to help them. First she would have to get herself out of this, and then she would see what could be done for those two. But there were always casualties in love and war.

Scar Face walked away from the two girls who were tied to the tree with Willow as she tried to reason with him again. "Look at me, Scar Face. Listen to me. I love you very much, and I will make my father listen to me so that we may be together. You really should take the girls back. I fear that this will not turn out in our favor. Put this in the past. The Great Spirit will show us which direction we are to take." She flashed him her biggest smile.

Scar Face looked at her through drunken eyes. "I want you. But I will not let those two leave. They will be a sacrifice tonight. If you wish you can join them." His voice was deadly cold, and his anger was directed at her. Willow caught her breath. She could see the warriors lighting the larger pile of wood, which caught quickly. She heard the crackling of the twigs and saw the two wooden stakes.

"Would you really do that to the one you love?" she asked.

Scar face sat down by the fire, making Willow sit next to him. He took off a piece of meat that had been roasting and offered her a piece of it, telling her, "I love you so much that if I can't have you then no one else will have you." With shaking hands she accepted the meat, taking a small bite and chewing it in her mouth until it tasted like sawdust. She wanted a little time before she had to respond to that last comment. This could go either way; in her favor or not.

"So, do you want me to stay here with you or will you let me go back?" she asked.

"If I let you go, how do I know you aren't going to run and tell everyone what has gone on? I think you are better off by my side."

Taking a swig of the firewater he lowered the jug, offering her a drink. "Do you want some?" he asked.

"Ah no. I'm fine right now."

He wasn't going to let her leave, and she would have to get herself out of this some way somehow. She felt trapped, and her stomach tightened, adding another knot. She was like the two who were tied to the tree—trapped.

Chapter Eleven

Amy ran outside to greet her grandma and grandpa, who were coming over for supper and also bringing Reid back home. Aunt Henrietta and Uncle Abe were coming in from town too. Charles walked in from the field with Carolyn next to him. She had a worried look on her face. The grandparents greeted the family.

"Have you seen the girls?" Carolyn asked them.

They looked at each other but shook their heads no.

"You lost them?" Henrietta asked with worried eyes.

"They went berry picking but should have been home by now," Amy chimed in.

"We should go look for them. Reid, come with us, son." Charles started to the barn but turned as he was walking. "They should have been back; it doesn't take that long to pick berries. If they are at the river or playing somewhere you will be taking back Katie with you, Abe and Henrietta. They need to learn responsibility."

"Charles, hop in the buckboard. We can all fit in here." Grandpa James moved over, and Reid jumped in the back of the wagon. Abe stayed on his horse. They turned around and started the search.

"We will see you in a little bit, Carolyn." Charles looked at her and clicked his tongue. The horses took off in a trot.

"Come on, Carolyn, Henrietta. Let's go in. Sitting out here isn't going to get the girls home any sooner." Grandma Ellen herded them all into the house.

"Amy, put on a spot of tea, would you, dear?" Grandma Ellen directed her.

Carolyn and Henrietta both turned to their mother. "Do you really want to read our tea leaves at a time like this?" Carolyn asked.

"My dear, what else would we do? Dinner is ready, right? Now get out the good teacups with the saucers. No one is to be expected to come over, and if they do we are drinking tea while the men get the girls back to us."

Carolyn set the four cups out, and Amy brought the water to boil. Grandma Ellen took the tea leaves out of a brown bag in the cupboard. While the water was boiling Grandma Ellen put the tea leaves in the bottom of the teapot and then poured in the hot water. As the tea seeped they all sat silently at the table.

"Ladies, place your hand slightly over the teacup. Now close your eyes and clear your thoughts. Please think of the question you so want answered today," Grandma Ellen directed the ladies.

"Carolyn, you may pour the tea now."

Carolyn got up and walked around the table, pouring tea water into each cup. She could see the tea leaves swirl out like a small eddy in a circle on the bottom of each cup. Grandma Ellen slowly sipped the hot beverage. Henrietta was trying to gulp hers but burned her tongue and the top of her mouth.

'Ouch, that is hot," she let them all know.

"Henrietta, please, we are all worried about girls. They will be home soon. Don't worry—the men will find them," Ellen assured her even if she was having some doubts herself.

Amy looked at Carolyn. "I thought we were not going to read tea leaves anymore."

Grandma Ellen's eyebrows rose up as she asked her question. "Yes, Carolyn, I would like to know that answer too."

"Desperate times call for desperate measures; we only do this when Grandma is here to supervise."

Grandma Ellen picked up where Carolyn left off. "Remember, ladies, any tea leaves that you get in your mouth place on the side of your saucer. You can either finish the tea till all the liquid is gone or drink as much of the tea as you possibly can. Okay, when you are done drinking your tea"—she showed them as she continued with her directions—"you pick up your cup and turn it upside down onto your saucer. Take your left hand. Please hold your saucer so it doesn't spin, and with your right hand spin your cup clockwise three times."

Amy was watching carefully; she didn't want to make a mistake. She had only been able to do this two other times with Grandma, her mom, and Selena. They didn't do it in front of the men or Reid. When all of them had their tea cups in position Grandma Ellen stood up and walked over to Henrietta's cup first.

Lifting the cup she took a hard look at the leaf shapes in the bottom of the cup. Henrietta could only see a bunch of little tea leaves, thinking to herself, *How can she make heads or tails out of that mess?*

"Henrietta, I see a beaver or an otter who is smiling. It is a male, not a female. He also is next to a single wolf, not one with a pack."

"What does that mean?" she asked.

"Shush, were not done yet," she scolded.

Next she picked up Carolyn's cup. It seemed to Amy along with the rest of them that it took an eternity for her to read the leaves. "Carolyn, I see a willow tree with a colorful bird sitting on it like the feathers in Selena's hat. There is a wolf looking at both. He must make a choice between the two."

Next Grandma Ellen went to Amy's cup. Amy could see that it was a tipi before Grandma could even say it. Amy whispered softly, "They are with the Indians, Grandma. They have been taken by the Indians."

"Amy, you did very well. You didn't think about it but spoke what you felt. You followed your inner child even if only a child yourself. Yes, I believe that they are with the Indians; where they are I do not know," Grandma Ellen answered quite firmly.

Grandma Ellen had made a full circle, and now she was back to her place at the table. Amy, Carolyn, and Henrietta's eyes were all on her, and the room was silent. She picked up her cup and flipped it over so she could see the leaves at the bottom. She brought it quickly up closer so she could look at the leaves better. Her hands start to shake and her color went pale. Her eyes mirrored the eyes looking back at her. The cup fell from her hand and crashed to the table, breaking into tiny pieces.

"Ma!" Carolyn screamed. "What did you see?"

Amy looked at her eyes. They were tearing up, with big tears about to flow over her bottom lashes. "What is it, Grandma?"

"Now girls, I didn't get that good of a look. My hands aren't as steady as they used to be, and the cup was still hot I really didn't get a good grip. Now Amy why don't you help your Aunt Henrietta clean up this mess."

Grandma Ellen got up and walked out the door of their small cabin. Carolyn followed behind, and Amy and Henrietta started to pick up the shattered teacup. It was past supper, and the evening was starting to set in.

"Ma, you might be able to fool the girls, but I know you saw what was in that cup," Carolyn said.

"Remember, our destinies are not set in stone. It depends on the path that is chosen. But since you asked, I will only say this once. Two went away, but only one shall return. It doesn't mean that any harm will be done, but one will return and the other not."

Carolyn swallowed hard, replaying the words in her mind. *One will return; one won't. That could mean almost anything. Oh please, Charles, bring home my baby.* She started to repeat the Lord's Prayer silently.

Charles, Abe, and Reid made good time to the berry patch. Charles stopped the team of horses, and the men and Reid got out and Abe got off his horse. They were calling for the girls.

"Pa, how come they aren't answering us?" Reid asked.

"It's okay, son. Selena, Katie, where are you?" The men continued to yell out their names.

"Look, Charles, there's a bucket. Don't go in there until we look at the tracks. It looks like moccasin footprints, and you can see where a struggle occurred." The men carefully picked their way through the bushes with Reid right on their tail. He spotted the new hat.

Reid pointed to the bushes, "Grandpa, there is Selena's hat. Look, it is all messed up."

Abe and Charles looked at each other. They knew that the girls had been there. It was getting dark, and they had followed the trail as far as they could.

Abe started pacing back and forth. "They will never be the same, Charles. They are with those heathens, and who knows what they are being put through. I should have never let Katie come."

"Abe, don't talk such nonsense. Our girls are survivors. They will put up a fight; don't you worry. We have gone as far as we can. Let's head back. It's getting dark, and we will need fresh horses. Reid, hop up in the wagon. We are going to go back to the farm."

"Abe, are you listening to me?" Charles looked at Abe. He knew that his brother-in-law was a little different and had issues. That is how he would explain it to folks who asked him. Abe just stared ahead, clenching his teeth along with his fists.

"I'm fine. I just do not want anything to happen to my daughter; that's all. There has been trouble recently with the natives," Abe said, still looking straight ahead.

Reid sat in the back of the wagon with tears running down his face. He was trying to be so strong and brave, but he was very tired along with being worried. He just wanted to go home. He wiped the tears with the back of his small hand, leaving a trail of tears mixed with dirt on his cheeks.

Chapter Twelve

Lone Wolf motioned to Laughing Otter as they squatted down by the edge of the woods.

"Why does Scar Face have the girls? Why is Willow here? What does she have to do with all of this?"

Lone Wolf was angry. "We need to get them out of here before they go to the sacrificial fire. How many of Scar Face's warriors are with him?"

"Only three," Laughing Otter replied.

"It looks like they have been drinking the white man's fire water. We should be able to take care of them easily enough."

Just as they were going to make their move they watched Willow mount up and ride off, following one of the warriors.

"Look, is Willow leaving?" Lone Wolf asked.

"It looks like two are left, including Scar Face, whom we have to take care of now that Willow is gone."

Lone Wolf looked back to the girls. They watched Scar Face walk to the tree. He bent down and, taking out his knife, cut Katie free. She struggled against him, but he dragged her toward the fire. He pushed her to the ground and kicked her hard in the ribs. Selena heard a thud as Katie screamed loudly; then silence. Katie lay where she had been kicked, motionless. The other warriors were still dancing around the burning blaze, drinking the firewater and not paying attention to what was taking place. The fire burned higher and higher, and tiny sparks were floating into the night air.

"You dirty bastard," Selena screamed at Scar Face. "You leave Katie alone." She was trying to get his attention.

While Selena had Scar Face's attention Lone Wolf and Laughing Otter went in different directions—first to take out the two dancing warriors and then to take care of Scar Face.

Scar Face stomped over to Selena, screaming at her, "You dirty white whore. You see what I did to your friend. You should see what I have in store for you." He grabbed her face and grinned as he tore off her dress from her shoulder down to her waist. Seeing the fear in her eyes he was suddenly filled with power.

Lone Wolf went behind the first warrior and with a quick slip of his knife to the warrior's throat watched him fall, as did the warrior Laughing Otter confronted. Lone Wolf turned just in time to see Scar Face attacking his Green Eyes. With a deep growl that came from the very depths of his soul he glared at them both. Still in the crouched position he sprang up to get to her. With Scar Face backside to him he didn't have to wait. Lone Wolf came up, grabbed Scar Face by the waist, and tackled him to the ground. Each was nearly as strong as the other, but Scar Face was stronger and seemed to have the advantage. All Selena could do was watch through teary eyes, her bottom lip and chin quivering. Not only were the two fighting, but they were doing battle not ten feet from her. Behind them she saw that the big blaze was out of control. It had jumped to the treetops, which were blazing with fire. The flames were jumping from treetop to treetop away from them, and the whole forest was soon to be on fire. Laughing Otter picked up poor Katie and carried her toward Selena. Lone Wolf and Scar Face were still going at it, knife to knife, in a battle by hand.

"We need to get out of here—the forest is on fire." Selena coughed as smoke started to choke her.

Using his knife, Laughing Otter cut Selena free. She got up and crawled to Katie, who still was unconscious. Laughing Otter went to help Lone Wolf only to see his knife enter into the chest cavity of Scar Face. Laughing Otter watched as the surprised look came across his face as Scar Face stumbled backward and with his hands reached for the knife.

"Brother, over a white face. You have taken my life over her." Scar Face exhaled a gurgled breath while a blood bubble exited his mouth. He glared at Lone Wolf and then went limp, and his dead eyes now stared straight ahead.

"It doesn't matter if she was white or not; you shouldn't have taken her," Lone Wolf replied as he wiped his blade off on the shirt Scar Face was wearing.

"Let's get out of here!" Selena's high-pitched scream brought him out of his stance. He ran to the tied-up horses that were wild-eyed from the fire burning all around them and led them with a rope. Selena met him with Laughing Otter carrying a limp Katie. Laughing Otter mounted up while Lone Wolf handed him Katie. He then jumped on his horse, and while his horse took off he swooped down and leaned over to pick up Selena. She landed safe in his arms, riding in front of him. She rode sideways on his horse with her head in the hollow of his shoulder. Lone Wolf's arms were strong and warm as he cradled her to himself.

No words were spoken. The race was on, and they needed to get to the river. It was their only chance. The wind had switched directions, and the fire was coming down the hillside right behind them. Selena could see animals running in the same direction as they were, trying to escape. She could see Katie's head bobbing up and down and back and forth even with Laughing Otter holding her as close as he could to his body, trying not to damage her ribs anymore than they were. Riding fast in the dark through the forest at breakneck speed would usually be suicidal, but the fire lit everything up as if it were daylight. Selena could hear the river before she could see it. Lone Wolf pulled his horse from a fast furious run to a dead stop. He jumped down, taking Selena with him. She landed on her feet, and Laughing Otter was right behind him.

He looked at Selena. "Do you trust me?" he yelled at her as he was trying to hold the horse down while it kept jumping straight up in the air to break free.

"What?"

"Do you trust me?" He looked right to the depths of her soul. Not waiting for her answer he tore the bottom of her skirt and ripped off a large piece of material. He tied it around the horse's eyes, and the horse calmed down. Selena didn't quite know what to think anymore. Her world had been torn upside down. She had gone from a crazy Scar Face back to Lone Wolf. A whinny from the other horse took her out of her thoughts.

Laughing Otter was trying to control his horse while holding onto Katie. The horse was spinning in circles with fright.

Lone Wolf grabbed Selena's hand and threw the rope at her. She knew what she needed to do, and she led the horse into the water. Lone Wolf got the other horse calm enough so Laughing Otter could dismount. While still holding Katie he carried her into the water to Selena and put her down in front of her. Selena wrapped her arms around Katie to hold her up. She then moved them into the water with only their heads showing. Katie, who was mumbling, now realized that she was very cold. She started to come to from the shock of the cold water. With a gasp she took in the night air, and the smoke filled her lungs. Her ribs protested from the expansion, and she quickly took little gasps of air instead, not wanting to start coughing.

"Katie, it's all right," Selena yelled to her over the crackling of the fire.

"Katie, I need to take off some of your dress so we can cover our faces from the smoke and heat," Lone Wolf yelled. He pulled out his knife. Selena could feel Katie stiffen up as he reached down to cut a large piece of dress off. He pulled it off, cut it in half, and gave them each a piece to cover their faces. The fire was directly above them now, and Selena could see a deer on the other side of the river. It was running like crazy in and out of the water, confused as to what it should do. Along with it some raccoons cowered on a log that was half in and half out of the water.

The fire blazed around them, and both men had their hands full with the horses. Selena was holding Katie in her arms when she suddenly heard a soft voice speak.

"Back in the river again—how did we end up back in the river again?" Katie spoke with hesitation and bewilderment.

"Yes, we are with Lone Wolf and Laughing Otter. They have once again saved us."

"They did? My ribs are killing me," she moaned.

The battle of the blaze continued above them. The first wave had gone by, and both girls had to duck under the water as it passed by, hoping that when they came up the air would be breathable—it was. Now the flames were still burning, but not as strong or as hot.

"Selena, I have decided that I'm not going to spend the night at your house anymore," Katie said, her teeth chattering. "I really just want to go home."

"Me too, Katie," Selena whispered to her while resting her chin on the top of her head. Both girls shivered through the night. Both were sore with aches and pains, but the cold water helped numb some of the pain. The ash covered their hair, and they had smudges all over their faces.

After the horses finally settled down, tired from the constant struggle, Lone Wolf went over to the girls.

"How are you doing?" All he could see were their white eyes against their soot-covered faces. They just continued to stare at him in bewilderment. He asked again, putting his hand on Selena's shoulder, "Are you okay?"

She nodded her head yes. Katie was going in and out of consciousness from shock along with the pain.

"We can get out of the water now, but before we do I should wrap Katie's ribs." Laughing Otter had now joined them. "It will be more comfortable to do in the water; she is weightless in here."

"I need to take more dress off," Lone Wolf announced as his knife cut the back of the bottom side off. He handed the long piece to Laughing Otter and gently wrapped it around Katie while Lone Wolf held her arms up. Lone Wolf carried Katie out of the water. Selena was concerned about her friend, but she couldn't help pout that her own cuts and bruises weren't attended to. They all remounted and rode off. Choosing their footing carefully between the smoldering brush and the charred ground the horses stepped gingerly. That was the last thing Selena would remember—the movement of the horse with the beating of Lone Wolf's heart as she lay against his chest. Her eyelids felt heavy and her arms and legs like rubber. She blinked quickly, trying to keep them open. Giving up the battle she then slowly closed them, and her eyes burned as her lids shut. She managed to open them slightly, looking up at the most handsome man she had ever seen. Feeling safe in his strong arms, she snuggled against him. She thought to herself, *Just need to close my eyes for a little bit.* She was they were so tired. She promised herself, *I will listen with my ears for danger. I will open my eyes back up if anything happens.* No sooner had she closed her eyes then she relaxed and was asleep.

Lone Wolf could tell by the rhythm of her breathing that she had finally succumbed to sleep. He knew she would be okay, but he didn't know about Katie. She was fragile, and it seemed that she had broken ribs and a rattle when she coughed. They needed to get them somewhere safe. Once Katie was stable then they would take the next step to bring them home. A slight grin came upon his face; his Green Eyes had much spirit. She would give him many strong sons someday.

They traveled through the rest of the night, heading to the cave where he had spent many days during his vision quest. It would be safe there. It was a place the fire had not reached.

They rode back up the mountain to the entrance of the cave. Lone Wolf woke up Selena and helped her down off the horse. When he walked to the back of the cave she followed. From a cache located at the bottom of the floor he took out a couple of bearskin rugs and laid them down. Laughing Otter was carrying Katie. He placed her down softly on them and removed what was left of her dress while covering her up.

"Selena, why don't you crawl in by Katie? We are going to get a small fire started and boil some water so you can wash up. There is some salve to place on your cuts."

Selena didn't hesitate. She didn't care that she was in her underclothing standing in front of two men. She just wanted to sleep. Exhaustion had taken its toll on her, and the day's events had finally caught up with her.

Both men had endured less sleep than this before when they had fought in a great battle. Laughing Otter started the fire and boiled water. Lone Wolf fetched extra clothes along with food staples and dried venison.

"I'm going back to our village. We were not in the direction of the fire, but someone should warn them about Scar Face." Laughing Otter spoke first, breaking the silence.

"All is well, my friend. I will see you tomorrow. Go with the Great Spirit." They nodded to each other, and Lone Wolf watched Laughing Otter leave on Katie's horse.

He checked on the girls and cleaned their faces while they slept. He applied salve to Katie's wounds along with her cuts. He was worried about her ribs, as her breathing was short and shallow as she slept. Selena, not the worst of the two, had a swollen cheek with a cut lip. Katie had a foot mark on her forehead where Scar Face had kicked her. Her hair was chopped short, but it would grow back, and she had broken ribs. Both girls shared similar rope marks and bruises on their wrists and arms where they had been tied to the tree. He shook his head, wondering why. Leaving the girls he moved to the front of the cave and, leaning against the wall, started to whittle a piece of wood.

Chapter Thirteen

Amy was watching the flames from the other side of the mountain with the other womenfolk.

"Do you think the menfolk got caught up in that fire?" Carolyn asked her mother.

"No, the berry patch is down the other side. I'm sure the girls didn't go that far."

"Listen. I hear a wagon, don't you?" Carolyn asked.

They all were squinting, but with it being dark out they could hear the wagon but not see it. As it came closer they moved down the steps of the porch to walk toward it. Henrietta ran to the wagon as it came up to the house.

"Are the girls with you?" she asked.

Reid jumped out and ran right to his mother's arms. "Mommy, Mommy the girls are gone." He shoved Selena's hat into her hands.

She wrapped him in her arms and rubbed her hands on the top of his head.

"Where are the girls?" she asked.

Charles answered for him as he got out of the wagon. "They were at the berry patch. It looks like they have had a run in with some natives and there was a struggle and they have been taken."

Abe now has his arms around his wife. Grandma Ellen was helping Grandpa unhitch the horses.

With a loud gasp, Henrietta looked up at her husband. "What do you mean taken?"

"Those dirty heathens! They took our daughter and will pay for taking her. I will find them if it kills me," he told his wife in an angered voice.

Sobbing was heard from Henrietta. Abe had his arm wrapped around her, but his face remained motionless. He was angry and in shock and was just going through the motions now.

"Let's get into the house so you can get ready to be on your way. Are you going to get Marshal Johnson?" Carolyn asked.

"Did you see the fire?" Amy asked her pa.

Abe yelled at her, "Yes, we did. Now get out of my way. We have to get ready to go." He stomped off away from them.

Charles looked at Amy, "Yes, we did see the flames and smelled the smoke." He gave Abe a strange look.

They walked into the house. Carolyn looked at Charles and saw his warm brown eyes filled with worry. He tried to smile but failed; it didn't reach his eyes. She caught her breath and knew that she needed to be strong. Charles reached for a warmer coat and grabbed one for Abe. Grandpa would stay behind this time along with Reid. Reid was sitting on the floor by the fire just staring at the flames. Amy was sitting by him. He was tired, and he leaned his head onto her shoulder as she wrapped her arms around him.

The men were ready in no time. Even if it was the wee hours of the night they were determined to get into town so they could start at first light.

Carolyn walked with Charles to the barn to saddle the horses. Once in the barn she took his hand and turned to him with beseeching eyes. "Charles, are they going to be okay?"

He squeezed her hand gently twice, a sign they had used for the many years of marriage. "We will find both girls. They are both strong young women, and they will be fine. The good Lord will look after both of them. We have our faith. It is now in his hands."

"I believe you, Charles, but that is our daughter out there. I know that she is alive. I feel it in my heart," she replied while she caught herself wringing her hands in her apron.

Charles had been saddling up his horse and was leading it out of the barn. Abe had his horse saddled. Looking angry, he bent down to kiss Henrietta on the head.

"Charles, are you ready to go?" Abe asked.

"Yes," Charles replied.

Grandpa James looked at them both along with Grandma Ellen, "Be careful. In only a couple more hours it will be daybreak. Don't worry about the womenfolk—I will be here with my shotgun." He patted the stock of the gun as he waved them off. They were a quiet bunch as they all walked back into the house; it was going to be a long couple of days.

Chapter Fourteen

Lone Wolf heard Selena before he saw her. The sun had just risen, and he had flatbread along with a jerky broth. He was kneeling and offering prayers of thankfulness to the Great Spirit. Selena was stiff along with being sore when she woke up. She put on the shirt that had been left by her side while she was asleep. It came down to her knees. It was big on her, but she had tied the waist with a piece of what was left of the ratty dress she had been wearing. She walked to the entrance of the cave and saw Lone Wolf kneeling with his arms outstretched in a meditative state. She stopped as the sun was rising, casting a glow on his bronze skin. He finished with his morning prayers and then looked up at her.

"How are you today?" he asked with a raised eyebrow. Now why was his Green Eyes dancing from foot to foot? She couldn't seem to stand still.

She answered, "I'm fine." She still looked past him into the woods as if searching for something or someone.

Lone Wolf looked behind him and saw no one. Was she in so much of a hurry to leave him?

"What are you looking at?" His curiosity was piqued.

Glancing down with her eyes lowered she moved her toe in a circle on the floor of the cave.

She slowly looked up at him, her cheeks pink. "I have to use the bathroom."

He just continued to stare at her, thinking to himself, *Why doesn't she just go? There are plenty of trees.*

As Selena was waiting for his response she tried a different approach. Maybe he didn't hear her or understand. "I have to make water; use the little girls' room." It was said in a tone that was a little louder, and her movements were quickening as she really had to go.

Lone Wolf smiled at her. "Are you going to stand there doing the pee dance or are you going to find a tree?" He pointed to a tree a few yards away.

With a huff of breath Selena glared at him but walked quickly by. She so wanted to stomp her foot, but she didn't have any shoes on. Walking away she found the first fir tree and relieved herself.

Coming back up to the cave she had every intention of ignoring this infuriating man. But she could smell the venison broth, and her stomach protested and won.

He handed her a bowl, and she sat down on the other side of the fire. He offered her a drink.

"Ouch." She brought her hand to her lip. "My lip hurts." She could feel the crack with her finger.

"I put healing salve on your cuts last night. They were much worse; I see some of the swelling has gone down."

"It hurts when I chew." She sipped slowly, drinking the broth. Oh, it felt so good to feel the warmness go through her, filling her tummy.

Both were sitting in silence in their own thoughts when suddenly a little wolf pup scrambled over the edge of the cave and ran to Lone Wolf. Selena couldn't help it; her mouth dropped open as she watched him pet the small wolf. Laughing Otter entered a few steps behind him.

She looked at each of them as they spoke in their native tongue. *How rude,* she thought. She cleared her throat, but the only one who paid any attention to her was the pup. He came over to where she was sitting and sniffed her knee. He looked up at her, and she reached down and let him sniff her hand and lick her fingers. She smiled, and he came over by her side, nudging his head under her arm. She gave him a piece of jerky, and he snapped it up with a couple of bites. She now had a new best friend, and he sat and looked at her. Lone Wolf had been watching the exchange from the corner of his eyes while he was talking. He smiled when he saw Selena sneak a piece of jerky to give to the pup, who was now lying on his back getting his belly scratched.

Laughing Otter had told everyone back at the village about what had happened. He also brought back supplies with him.

Selena heard a soft voice calling out her name; it was Katie.

Selena got up as fast as she could and went over to Katie. Kneeling next to her and bending closer she could see that Katie's eyes were open. "Are you okay? Are you hurting?" she asked.

"Yes to both," Katie whispered. "But I really need to go to the bathroom."

Just then Laughing Otter cleared his throat. He was standing behind Selena, and the girls hadn't heard him walk to them.

"I brought back a couple of dresses if you want to change," he told them. Feeling awkward he quickly placed the dresses in Selena's lap and turned and walked back out to Lone Wolf.

"Well, let's get you into one of these dresses. Then I will help you get outside."

It took a little bit and an ouch or two, but soon they each had on a doeskin dress. Katie was leaning on Selena heavily as they limped out to the entrance. Lone Wolf looked up. Selena had braided her hair. If it were not blonde she would look no different from the maidens back home.

Laughing Otter asked Lone Wolf in their native language, "Why are they standing there staring at us, and how come Katie is shifting from foot to foot?"

Lone Wolf smiled. "I call it the pee tree dance. I don't understand why the white women just don't go relieve themselves behind a tree or bush but feel they have to announce what they are doing." He chuckled.

Selena didn't understand the language, but she knew what they were talking about. She lifted her chin up high. Her pride wanted her to walk out and not come back. But she glared at Lone Wolf as they walked by.

"Selena, slow down. I can't walk that fast. My ribs are killing me," Katie begged.

"Sorry, Katie. I will explain later. I will help you, and then you should try to eat something," Selena told her.

When the girls came back, Katie gently sat down on a piece of wood that Laughing Otter had brought over from the woodpile. It would be easier for her to get up from there than from the ground. She was handed a bowl of broth, which she sipped slowly.

Chapter Fifteen

Morning had come to the farm, but no one had slept that night. Amy came down from the loft. She could smell the coffee her Ma had made. Grandma, Grandpa, and Aunt Henrietta were all sitting at the table with their hands wrapped around cups of coffee. No one was talking. They were just sitting there lost in their own thoughts.

"Morning," Amy softly spoke.

Her mom looked up and saw the dark circles under her eyes. "Good morning Amy. Would you gather the eggs please?" she asked.

"I'll help you," Reid chimed in as he got up from the chair he was sitting on. Both tried to get out the door at the same time, but Reid, the smaller of the two, made it out first.

The adults could hear the yells from the outside.

"Pa, you're back!" Amy yelled.

Reaching the door they saw Charles, Abe, Marshal Johnson, and his two sons.

"Morning, ladies." Marshal Johnson tipped his hat.

"We're not staying long," Abe stated. He looked worn out and a little on edge, his hand constantly placed on his holstered pistol.

"Charles, we have extra saddle bags packed for when you find the girls." Carolyn leaned up to hand him the bags, as he was still mounted on his horse.

"Did anyone hear how the fire was started?" Henrietta asked, breaking the silence.

"Crazy Pete said he had spotted some Indians going up the other side of the mountain. It looked like they had two white girls with them. He had been coming down from where they were headed. That's where the fire started." The marshal filled them in and told them that Crazy Pete had seen a huge fire waiting to be lit with two stakes placed in the middle. He didn't want to stick around to see what was going to happen.

Abe glared at the marshal, "Stop talking now. No need to scare the womenfolk. We need to get going. I want my daughter back, not damaged goods; they are with those heathens," he scolded back.

Grandma Ellen looked at Grandpa James and shook her head to herself. "Abe, you don't know what or how the girls are. You should think positive," she replied.

Abe turned his hated look on Ellen. "Mind your own business. I didn't want this to happen, but I can't change it now, can I!"

Charles looked at Carolyn. "Don't worry about the girls. We will find them and bring them both home. Amy, Reid, mind your ma now. Reid, you need to take care of the livestock, you hear?" Charles gave out his orders along with a nod of his head.

"Yes, Pa." Reid stood a little taller, and Amy nodded her head in agreement.

"Henrietta, you can stay here. Don't you go anywhere. I have the store taken care of," Abe ordered her.

"I will stay here, Abe."

"Well, folks, this is all nice, but we need to go," Marshal Johnson told them.

"We're heading back to the farm for a little bit, Carolyn," Grandpa James told her. "We need to get back but will ride over in a day or two."

Looking at Reid, he said, "Son you need to be strong now." He rested his hand on Reid's shoulder he gently squeezed it. "Keep the womenfolk safe. Now I don't know why your sister and Katie have been taken. It doesn't make much sense, but stay close to the farm."

Chapter Sixteen

Katie was still sipping her broth while Selena was petting the little wolf pup. He let her rub his belly and then gently nipped her hand. An uncomfortable silence was now about them as they sat by the fire lost in their own thoughts.

Selena broke the silence first. Not one to mince words, she could be straight to the point. "So why were we captured? When can we go home?"

"Why did they cut my hair? And who was that awful man with the scar on his face?" Katie reached up to touch her short hair. Her hand shook, her complexion still pale.

Lone Wolf looked at them both, choosing his words carefully.

"The warrior who took you was Scar Face. He was in love with the young woman you saw last night. Her name is Willow. The two tribes wanted to join together as one with an arranged marriage. Willow and I are to join together on the new moon."

That caught Selena's attention, and her eyes narrowed a little as she looked at him. Katie looked at her friend and could see that she had too much interest on her face. Could she really be falling for Lone Wolf?

"Well, that's all fine and dandy, but what does that have to do with Katie and me?" Selena demanded.

"I can answer that question." Laughing Otter had been silent until that point. "When I went back to the village I found that after Willow was escorted back home she went to her father, Chief White Cloud, to tell him what happened. It seems that Scar Face had seen us with you two the other day at the river. He had also seen Willow and Lone Wolf talking the other night at the fire and he didn't like it at all. So he thought he would frame Lone Wolf by capturing you two and sacrificing you both. When the white men found out there would be hell to pay and the peace between our villages would be shaken. Scar Face had planned to

64

leave signs that would lead to Chief Two Timber's village so that trouble would be made for us and the marriage would be called off. The one thing Chief White Cloud does not want is any trouble with the white folk. Then Willow and Scar Face could be free to marry, and who would know any different?"

When Laughing Otter finished both girls turned and looked right at Lone Wolf, who was using a stick to move the hot coals around in the fire. Not one to avoid conflict, Lone Wolf chose his words carefully. He could feel their eyes on him.

"I did know that Scar Face and Willow had feelings for each other. I was not part of any of this until we came to the berry patch looking for that bear and found a hat and your footprints. Once again we came to your rescue," Lone Wolf reminded Selena.

"So that's all honky dory, but we really want to go home now." Selena glared at Lone Wolf, and her body language said it all.

"You will when Katie is able to move more easily. Right now it would be too painful for her," he replied, his voice much louder than hers.

"Well, can't we send word to our ma and pa that we are okay? They must be wondering what happened to us," Katie pleaded.

"We will leave tomorrow or the next day. Tensions are high right now, and the time it would take Laughing Otter or me to go to tell them would only delay our leaving. Plus your parents would want to come back with us to retrieve you. No one who isn't a descendent of our great fathers is allowed on the sacred land. It would make more sense to just wait a day or two and then travel home."

"I guess you are right. What is a day or two? We are safe. They will be worried, but if they knew we were out here with you it would just stir up trouble." Katie agreed with Lone Wolf. "Selena, if you would help me I would like to lie down for a while. I'm exhausted right now."

Selena looked at Katie and saw that her complexion was whiter than when they first came out. She looked like she was ready to fall asleep right there by the fire. Standing up, she helped Katie back into the cave to rest for a while.

Katie was tucked in the bear rug bedding, which was very soft, and she looked up at Selena. "I'm sorry I'm not able to travel right now. I know you want to go home, because I do. But I'm more worried about the way you are looking at Lone Wolf, Selena. He is off limits. You know how people are around here. They wouldn't stop talking for a month of Sundays. Selena, it won't be allowed."

"I know, but he isn't like the boys our age." Selena knelt down by Katie. Even though it was dark in the back of the cave, Katie could see Selena's eyes sparkle as she spoke. "I don't know if he even likes me. Just look at me—I'm in a doeskin dress, my hair needs washing, and I would really like to go dip in the water."

She looked at Katie, whose eyelids were heavy and whose breathing had slowed to a sleepy stage. Blinking her eyes she smiled at Selena. "You will do what your heart tells you to do. Go see if there is a place to wash up. It must be close, because I saw Laughing Otter with a pail of water not too long ago."

Selena walked out to the entrance of the cave. Lone Wolf wasn't there, but Laughing Otter was putting more wood on the fire.

"Laughing Otter, is there a river nearby? I would really like to clean up a little better," Selena said.

Pointing to the trail that led from the opening of the cave Laughing Otter continued to explain the way to the waterfall; it was not that far away. "Go a couple yards from the cave where there is a sharp corner. Then turn to the left and go between the two fir trees. If you look up you will see a scarred willow tree. Go to it and you will hear the water flowing; there is a waterfall. It pools downstream, but there is a place where you can swim and wash up. Lone Wolf is looking for game and shouldn't be too long. Do you want to wait?"

Selena shook her head. "No, I can find it. I promise not to be too long." Looking straight into his eyes, she asked, "It is safe, isn't it?"

"Yes, you have no fear in this land. You are under the protection of myself and Lone Wolf." He bent down and picked up a little pouch that he then tied around her neck. It fell between her breasts. "Lone Wolf thought you would want to explore. You are one of us now."

Looking down, she took her hand and held the little pouch with tiny fringes on it. She just smiled and walked to the edge of the cave. Her dress fit her body perfectly, her blonde hair was in braids, and tiny freckles were lightly sprinkled on her nose. "Thanks, Laughing Otter. I promise not to get in any trouble." She smiled turned and walked away. "Oh, will you watch Katie for me?" She left but thought she heard him mumble something about how come he had to be the one left at the cave. That made her smile.

Walking down the trail she saw the two fir trees and looking up found the scarred willow tree. Thinking to herself, *He gave good directions,* she could hear the water as it cascaded and splashed at the bottom of the falls.

Selena found a place to enter into the clearing. She looked around. The birds were chirping everything seemed to be safe as far as she could tell, but it was hard to know with the water flowing. But once again she didn't realize that Lone Wolf was doing the same thing she was on the other side of the falls.

Chapter Seventeen

Lone Wolf didn't know that Selena was at the falls. He had come to wash. He had not been successful hunting but wanted to be clean. With his instinct always on alert he turned to see Selena just as she was going to take off her dress. He swallowed. As if putting on a show just for him she slowly lifted her arms, pulling the dress over her head. She was blonde everywhere, and her breasts were round and firm. He had seen her before, and the memory was etched in his mind. But again even in the cold water his manhood was starting to have a mind of its own. Her hair was out of its braids, and the sun made it glow. She gently touched the water with her toes and shivered but continued to walk in. Goose bumps arose all over her body as she slowing walked into the water until it reached her lower part. It was very cold, and with a gasp of air she continued to walk in. Her nipples were now standing at attention. They were proud and hard and begging to be touched. That's when she dove under the water, swimming underneath only to reappear again, flipping her hair out of her face. Lone Wolf thought to himself that she was like a water spirit. Selena, not knowing that she was being watched, tread water and then lay on her back to float, letting the water just swirl around her. The sun was up high in the blue sky, with only a cloud here and there; what a peaceful place to be. Brought out of her daydream, she felt something touch her bottom. She quickly went back to treading water, looking to the left and then right. She was starting back to shore when she felt a tug on her hand. Turning around, she was ready to do battle. She came face to face with Lone Wolf. There he was, the most handsome man she had ever seen. His brown eyes spoke words of mischief along with his lip, which turned up with a smirk. *Oh, he knows I don't have anything on,* she thought to herself.

"Oh, I didn't know anyone was here," she stammered at him as she continued to swim toward the bank but then remembered that she didn't have a stitch on. She covered her chest with her hands. He smiled at her, and her heart fluttered. She was starting to have feelings that she had never felt before, and her cheeks blushed as she put her chin down.

"If you would be ever so kind to turn around I will get out of the water so you can continue doing whatever it was until I bothered you."

"What's the hurry? Stay and swim with me." He took a step closer. His chest had tiny water drops all over it.

When she was finally able to touch the bottom and get her footing she turned and looked straight at him. "You really need to be going now."

"I think I have found something much more interesting," he replied.

She could feel his breath on her forehead. *Do I dare look up?* Selena thought to herself. Against her wishes she did, only to look straight into his eyes. He bent slowly down toward her. She couldn't move her feet from where they were planted. Just as she thought he was going to kiss her he stopped just inches from her face.

"Come with me. I want to show you something behind the water fall. Or are you afraid, Green Eyes?" he challenged her.

Selena mumbled to herself, "Said the spider to the fly." She knew better. She should just turn back to shore and get her dress on and go back to the cave. But part of her wanted to go with him.

Lone Wolf could see that she was trying to decide what to do. Her emotions were playing across her face. His voice was as smooth as honey. "That is unless you are too afraid." Fiery eyes glared at him, making her eyes turn a shade greener.

"I'm not afraid. What is it you want to show me?" She turned, facing the falls, and raised her chin higher. He dove forward, leaving her behind. Being a strong swimmer herself, she followed him as he swam to the side of the falls. She hesitated for a second as she saw him dive under. *What the heck?* She took a deep breath and followed. With eyes open she could see him ahead of her and felt that the current was fast, but she just swam harder than she ever had before. They both come up for air at the same time. They were in a small cave behind the fall. On the wall she could see drawings from the visitors before them. But the most amazing was all of the butterflies that were in there. Selena had never seen that many before or so many different kinds.

Lone Wolf swam over to the edge and lifted himself up. Selena could see his bronzed back and white cheeks. Oh, I should turn away. He walked ever so proudly away and came back dressed and holding a blanket.

He smiled at her, "Would you like me to hold it for you, or do you want me to put it down so you can wrap up in it."

"Put it down. I will wrap up—and turn around," Selena scolded him.

Selena picked up the blanket. It barely covered her from her breasts to her butt. She figured that as long as she didn't sit down, it wouldn't get too breezy. Still, her ma would die of shock if she could see her now.

Lone Wolf turned toward her. "Many of my tribal members have come to the sacred cave. They drew their story on the walls."

"Have you left a story, Lone Wolf?" she asked.

"I haven't felt it in my heart to leave behind a special one. Would you like to?" He bent to pick up a black charcoal-looking rock.

"Yes, I would." Selena found an empty space on the cave wall. She started to draw. Lone Wolf left her to make a small fire. When he was done he noticed that she was just standing there looking at her work. He walked up behind her but drew in a breath when he saw what she had drawn: a willow tree and a bird of the different color—the same colors that he seen on the hat at the berry bush—with a wolf below it. But he noticed that in the next scene the bird was on the back of the wolf. How could his Green Eyes know of his vision?

Selena looked up at him. "Is it that bad?"

"No, I have just seen it before."

"Really? Where? I just drew what I felt." His eyes softened he took the stone out of her hand. He lifted her chin up with his fingers and bent down and slowly kissed her gently on the lips. Not sure what to do, she mimicked his lips and returned the kiss. With a muffled groan he reached behind her and pulled her closer into his arms. She felt his hard chest as her hands fell against him. With a surprise her mouth opened slowly, and his tongue entered.

He picked her up and carried her to the fire, laying her down with him. He deepened his kiss, cupping his hand around her cheek and kissing her face, and she moaned. He lovingly bit her neck, trailing kisses toward her collar bone. She watched his hand slowly open the blanket and gasped as the cold air touched her. Selena felt a shock go through her entire body as her back arched up toward him. Hearing a noise, she realized that it was herself she was hearing. She didn't notice that the blanket had been opened all the way until she felt his warm hand on her stomach. She clenched a little bit, but he gently moved her legs. Suddenly she felt something hard enter her wetness, and as he pushed she felt a sharp pain. After the pain subsided the pleasure followed. It was so intense that feelings came crashing over her, and she screamed with delight as he drove his manhood into her until he couldn't hold back any longer. From above she opened her eyes to look at Lone Wolf. His eyes are glazed over with desire as waves of passion crashed over him.

Chapter Eighteen

Charles and Abe had been on the road for a couple of nights along with the rest of the posse. With the trail ending up where the fire looked to have been started it didn't look very promising. They stood around what was left of the fire pit with the two charcoal posts burned to the ground.

"Now, Abe, it doesn't mean anything," Charles informed his brother-in-law.

"How do ya know that? We followed as best as we could up to this here fire pit. You know as well as I do what those stakes are for, and there are two of them," Abe yelled back, pacing back and forth. He was a mild-mannered man under normal circumstances, but the stress of Katie being gone had turned him into a different person.

"Abe, there aren't any bones. Even with the fire getting out of control there would be some kind of sign of the girls," Marshal Johnson tried to reassure him.

Abe looked at the men. Then he looked around, noticing that everything was all black and charred from the fire. Even if the girls weren't there, how could they have survived the fire? This was just awful, and he shook his head back and forth as his shoulders slumped over.

"I know it's been a couple of days, but we will find them," the marshal tried to reassure him, but his words sounded hollow even in his own ears.

"Let's get out of here before evening sets. Maybe we can pick up their trail tomorrow." The Johnson boys followed their pa's orders, as did Charles, and single file they rode out of the charred mess. Abe was the last to leave. The smell of smoke was still in the air as some of the logs were still smoldering.

Riding away, the men were quiet, but Charles could hear Abe mumbling under his breath about the no-good heathens that took his daughter and how they were going to pay for it. Dirty filthy Indians. How dare they take his Katie, his only child? They would all pay.

Later on that night the men ate and washed the food down with some good black coffee; that is, everyone but Abe.

Marshal Johnson looked at Charles. "Is he okay?" He glanced at Abe.

"I don't know. I haven't seen him like this before. I know he can be different and all, but I have never seen him like this," Charles answered.

Both men looked over to where Abe was sitting. They could see him cleaning and wiping his pistol over and over again, not really talking to the others but just wiping his pistol while staring into the fire. Charles was afraid that he was losing his mind or the battle that seemed to be raging within him.

"Better keep an eye on Abe. Who knows what condition we will find the girls in, I'm sorry to say, Charles. I know Selena is out there too." The marshal stood up to dump the remainder of his coffee into the fire. It hissed its complaint. They all turned in for the night, each wrapping up in their bedrolls, except Abe, who was still feeding the fire and clutching his gun.

Charles looked up into the sky at all the stars, thinking of his daughter, just like one of the tiny stars in the sky among all the other stars around her. How would they ever find them?

Unbeknownst to Charles, Carolyn was standing on their porch back home, wrapped up in her shawl, leaning against the railing, looking up at the sky and wondering where her daughter and niece were and whether her husband was close to finding them both.

Dear Lord, please watch over my family, Carolyn prayed. *Please spread your loving kindness over them all. Guide them all safely back into our arms safe and sound.* She ended her prayers with the sign of the cross and turned and walked back into the house.

Chapter Nineteen

Two days later Katie took a turn for the worse, and it was time for the girls to start their journey back home. The native medicine stabilized her, but she needed to get to the white man's doctor.

"Katie will ride with Laughing Otter. Selena can ride her horse behind me," Lone Wolf announced the next morning as they were getting ready to leave.

Selena had been very quiet. She sat on her horse bareback with her Indian dress on, her hair braided.

Katie could feel Laughing Otter's breath on her neck as they rode. She was sitting in front of him, and he supported her with his arm. They had become friends, but that was it. Laughing Otter was proud of his son and wife who were back at home. Katie had thought differently of the natives since she spent a couple of days with them.

Lone Wolf could tell that Selena was in deep thought. She was concentrating very hard. She needed to learn to let the Great Spirit guide her on the road she would travel. They would be together one way or another—he felt it in his heart.

Selena knew that she was in love with Lone Wolf. Her mother and father, on the other hand, might not see eye to eye on the subject, even if they did believe in true love. Just how was she going to tell them all of this? Another worry was what if she was with child. Her hand came to rest on her flat stomach.

Lone Wolf and his party were coming down the mountain while Marshal Johnson and his party were going up.

Marshal Johnson had just told the boys to go up the other trail to see if there were any sign of the girls. He, Charles, and Abe took the other fork on the trail. Charles spotted them first. He caught a glimpse of something or someone coming down the hill. They dismounted and tied up their horses and positioned themselves behind a windfall and a large rock. Charles could see Selena's horse as they got closer and could see that she was wearing a doeskin dress and had braided hair. There was another horse with two riders on it. Abe whispered to Charles that he thought Katie was riding with a heathen Indian, and why was her hair cut short?

"Abe, now we don't know what's going on. Katie is riding with one of the natives, but Selena is as good a rider as any boy I have seen, and she is riding Spirit. She could have gotten away any time but hasn't." Charles held Abe back.

"Well, that may be all true, but maybe she won't leave Katie. Why isn't she riding her horse?" he asked angrily.

"Well, they are coming our way. Just don't go shooting until we find out what is going on. Do you hear me, Abe?" Marshal Johnson looked at them both.

Lone Wolf felt rather than saw the trap that had been set. He could have dodged it, but Laughing Otter had Katie and Selena was riding right behind him. He spoke in his native language sharply to Laughing Otter. Katie sat up straight—something wasn't right.

Marshal Johnson stood up, pointing his gun at them. "Stop where you are!" Click, Click; the other two cocked their guns.

"Pa, is that you?" Selena held her hand above her eyes. "Pa, it is you!" Lone Wolf looked from Selena to her father. He could see the resemblance.

Charles looked at his daughter. He had never seen her dressed like that. Her face looked like it had been bruised, but other than that she looked okay. His heart started pounding. His daughter was right there in front of him.

Before anyone could blink or move an eye Abe jumped out from behind the windfall, pointing his gun at Laughing Otter. "Get your filthy hands off my daughter. Release her now," he yelled.

"Abe, put your weapon down. They haven't even drawn any of their weapons," Marshal Johnson warned.

"Pa, Pa, it's me, Katie. I'm okay. We were taken by some bad Indians." Before she could finish Abe shot his gun in the air above their heads. The horses shied away, throwing Katie off and taking Laughing Otter with her to the ground.

Marshal Johnson jumped out from behind the rock, pointing his gun at Abe. "Put the gun down right now, Abe, before you shoot someone."

Abe just stood there glaring at the marshal. Charles had never seen Abe act like that; neither had Selena or Katie. Abe had lost his mind.

"Uncle Abe, stop it right now!" Selena found her voice as Spirit pranced back and forth. Lone Wolf had his knife in hand.

Laughing Otter had fallen next to Katie when the horse spooked. He stood up first. When he went to reach down to offer his hand to Katie Abe pointed his gun at them both. "I said get your filthy hands off my daughter, you savage beast. I will shoot you; I will." His hand was deathly still as he pointed the gun at Laughing Otter.

As Katie managed to get up on her own, Laughing Otter was backing up and Lone Wolf was getting ready to throw his knife. The tension was thick.

"Put your gun down." Lone Wolf took the men by surprise as he spoke in perfect English. "We mean you no harm."

Laughing Otter reached for Katie. He could see she was shook up and not at all steady on her feet. Katie watched as her father pointed the gun right at Laughing Otter. She knew he was going to pull the trigger.

Screaming out "No!" she jumped up in front of Laughing Otter just as the hammer came down and the bullet left the chamber. The impact of the bullet slammed her into Laughing Otter, and both went down to the ground again.

Selena screamed Katie's name as she jumped from her horse.

Lone Wolf threw his knife. It caught Abe in his shoulder a second too late.

Selena reached Katie and slid to the ground beside her, lifting her head onto her lap and putting pressure on the wound in her chest, trying to stop the flow of blood. Selena looked at Katie's chest. It had a gaping hole, and crimson red was spreading all over Katie's front. She was coughing with a gurgling sound as blood seeped out of the corner of her mouth.

Crying hysterically, Selena placed her hand on Katie's chest, "Katie, please don't leave me. Hang on; it's going to be okay." She looked up to see her father ripping off his shirt. Lone Wolf was trying to stop the blood with his hand also while Laughing Otter dug through his medicine bag. Abe knelt beside Katie, looking around at the blood-soaked ground.

"Oh Katie, my dear Katie. I'm so sorry. Please forgive me, daughter. Don't leave me, please." Tears were rolling down his face.

Katie couldn't feel the hard ground beneath her anymore. She was now so cold. Why so cold? The pain was not as it had been before. She opened her eyes and was going to ask if she was okay, but she read the answers written on the faces that were looking down at her—she wasn't going to make it out of this one. She had known all along that she would only be here a short time before she went home to the good Lord.

"Pa?" she tried to speak with a strong voice, but only a whisper was heard.

Still kneeling down he leaned closer to Katie. "Yes, daughter, I'm here. I've got your hand, honey. Hold on. You're going to make it." With a choking voice, he pleaded, "I'm so sorry, Katie. I didn't mean for it to hit you. Oh God, Katie, please forgive me." He cried his tears openly in front of all to see, his shoulders slouched over, a defeated man.

Katie raised her hand and placed it on the side of his face. "Pa, I love you. Tell Ma I love her too. It wasn't your fault, Pa. A life for a life, Pa. Remember: a life for a life." Katie was remembering how Laughing Otter had saved her from drowning earlier.

Selena's tears fell on Katie's face, and her eyes burned. Her stomach felt as if she was going to throw up. Katie still lay with her head in Selena's lap and looked up at her. Selena could see the life slipping from Katie's eyes as the grayish-white color took over. She bent down to Katie, who whispered her last words to her, "Remember to follow your heart, Selena."

"I will! I promise I will, Katie. Hold on. You can make it. You have been through worse things than this. Hold on. Please!" Selena sobbed.

Katie eyes stared at Selena, her pupils fixed. Then the last breath left her body and she went limp. Katie was on her way to a new journey. She was now a free spirit. Her soul had left her body, and she hovered above them all, only to see everyone leaning over her lifeless body.

"Katie! Oh God, Katie! Please no! Don't leave me. Please don't go!" Selena screamed, shaking her head back and forth.

Abe staggered up and looked around at the scene before him. His daughter was gone, and her life seeped into the earth where she lay. He felt the pain in his shoulder as he pulled out the knife and threw it on the ground. All eyes were upon him.

With tears streaming down his face he looked from face to face. "I didn't mean it; I didn't shoot her. She jumped in the way." His hand reached down for his pistol and hovered over the handle. His body was twitching like he couldn't stand still.

"Abe, settle down. We all saw what happened and know it was an accident. You didn't mean to do it. Katie jumped in the way to save him." He pointed to Laughing Otter. The marshal spoke calmly, starting to walk toward Abe.

Abe, continuing to walk away from them backward, pulled his gun out and waved it at them. He took a couple of steps backward and stumbled but regained his footing. "I didn't shoot her. I didn't mean to. You have to believe me!"

"Abe, put the gun down. It's okay; accidents happen." Marshal Johnson took a step toward him.

Selena leaned over and kissed Katie on the forehead. "I love you, Katie. You were always a sister to me." She took Lone Wolf's knife and cut a piece of Katie's hair off and put it in the leather pouch that now hung from her neck. She looked at her hands. They were covered with Katie's blood, and her dress was soaked with it. Her legs felt weak as she wavered, but Lone Wolf caught her arm. Her pa was trying to get Uncle Able to settle down before he shot someone else. Since all eyes were on Uncle Abe, Selena, Lone Wolf, and Laughing Otter backed up to their horses and mounted up.

"Where are you going? Get off that horse, you tramp," Abe yelled at her. "All because of you my Katie is dead. You always got her into trouble. Well, you won't forget this time now, will you, Selena? Why should you live when she died?"

Selena watched in disbelief as her uncle pointed his gun at her. Lone Wolf was just going to react when Abe changed direction and placed it next to his temple. With no warning he looked at them all, smiled, and pulled the trigger and then folded to the ground.

All Selena could hear was screaming. She was wondering who was doing all that screaming when she realized that it was herself. Charles ran to Abe, as did Marshal Johnson. The Johnson boys were just coming around the bend in the road when they saw Abe end his life. They both just sat there motionless, trying to take in all they had just seen plus a dead Katie on the ground and Selena riding behind an Indian soaked in blood.

Charles stopped and turned. There was nothing he could do for Abe. Enough tragedy and disaster had taken place for one day, and he just wanted his daughter to be safe and to come home with him. He watched Marshal Johnson cover what was left of Abe's upper body with a jacket. He looked at Selena, who somehow looked older, braver.

"Selena, please." He looked at Lone Wolf.

"His name is Lone Wolf, and he and Laughing Otter saved us from a mean Indian named Scar Face. If it weren't for them, Pa, I would be dead. Do you hear me? Dead. That is what Katie was talking about—a life for a life. They saved ours, and she saved Laughing Otter's; a life for a life," Selena looked right into her father's eyes.

Charles, always the level-headed one, knew that this was going to be tricky. He could tell that his daughter didn't trust anyone right then except that big

Indian Lone Wolf, who was holding her against him protectively on his horse. It didn't look like he was going to release her anytime soon.

"Please, Selena, will you come down so we can talk? Your ma misses you something fierce, and it's time for you to come home now," her father pleaded with her.

Selena felt her heart melt a little. Then she glanced down at her hands, which were dry and crusted with her best friend's blood. Looking at the lifeless body of Katie, she told herself, *You were right. Katie. I'm going to follow my heart.*

"No, Pa. I'm with Lone Wolf now. Tell Ma, Reid, and Amy that I love them all and will be along to say hi, but I don't want to go with you. I'm going home with the man I love." She leaned her head back into Lone Wolf's chest, and he tightened his arm around her waist.

Marshal Johnson could see Charles's shoulders slump in defeat. He wasn't going to win this one. "Charles, if we force this, there could be more deaths," he told him.

Looking back at the marshal, Charles replied, "I want her to come back with us where she belongs." He spoke to his daughter, "Come home with us."

Lone Wolf answered for her, "Selena is free to come and go as she pleases. She can visit when she feels safe, or you may come to us. You are now under the protection of my father, Chief Two Timbers. We live in the valley below."

"Selena, we love you, honey. Please come back to us." Charles tried one more time.

"No, Pa, we're leaving now. Please don't make this harder than it already is. Tell Ma that I will see her soon." She looked back at Lone Wolf, and they turned and left.

"Boys." Marshal Johnson looked at his own sons, both a shade whiter than he had ever seen them. "Get Abe's bedroll so we can wrap up what is left of him. We will put him up on his horse." The boys just stared at him. He walked over to the horse and retrieved the blanket. Charles was doing the same with his bedroll for Katie. After the bodies were both wrapped and placed on the back of the horse they started on their way home.

A sad bunch they were, quiet as could be. You could only hear the clip clop of the horse's hooves when they hit a stone here and there. Each was deep in his own thoughts. Each was replaying what had taken place or how it could have been changed.

Lone Wolf and Laughing Otter were just as quiet riding back to the village. Selena either passed out or just shut down from everything that had just taken place. All she kept saying to herself in her voice within her mind was *Katie is dead. I can't believe it—Katie is dead. How could this have happened? Katie is gone. This must be a nightmare. I know I'm going to wake up.* But every time she closed her eyes she could see Katie jumping in front of Laughing Otter. She could see the blood filling the front of her dress with Katie laying her head on her lap, taking her last breath, and then she was gone.

They came to the village after only a stop or two. Lone Wolf took care of Selena, and they stopped by a stream to try to wash most of the blood from her hands and arms. She walked into the stream with her dress on. The water ran red with Katie's blood. Most came out, but the stain would be there forever, like the one on her heart.

Chapter Twenty

They entered the village later that night. Most of the villagers were curious about the white woman Lone Wolf was carrying in his arms. But one look at the intensity in the eyes and even the nosiest of the bunch didn't dare ask any questions.

Lone Wolf entered his tipi first and went over to his furs and laid her down. He wrapped her in furs and got her something to drink.

She opened her eyes to see the stars peeking in from the top of the tipi, thinking to herself that it looked like when she looked out her window at home. It seemed like such a long time ago; how can your life change so quickly? A rough little tongue licked her hand, bringing her back to the moment, and a head nuzzled her arm. It was Wolf, the pup. He had found his way back home. She scratched his head with her fingers as he laid his head on his two front paws and looked at her. "I know; I'm going to miss her too." She just continued to stroke his fur.

Lone Wolf was sitting next to her. "I'm going to my father's tipi. You will be safe here. No one dares enter or harm anyone who is under my protection. Wolf will keep you company." He kissed her on the cheek, and she smiled at him. "I just want to sleep now." She closed her eyes and tried to go to sleep. But the events of the day played havoc in her mind; the vision of Katie's breathing her last breath would haunt her forever. Hot tears seeped from her clenched closed eyes to roll down each side of her face. Wolf whimpered a soulful cry. As he belly-crawled up to her face she could feel him dry her tears with his rough tongue.

Lone Wolf changed into different clothes and gathered up the old clothes and headed out. He went to the medicine woman, who took the clothes. She would know how to take care of them; they still had the spirit of Katie's life on them. He just nodded his head. No words were needed with the medicine woman. She knew, and he kept on walking. He saw Laughing Otter with his arms wrapped around his wife's shoulder and a little boy tugging at his leg. He stopped mid-stride. Katie had known that Laughing Otter had a family and a little one. She took his place so that Laughing Otter would have many more moons with his wife and his son, not to mention the one on the way. Many a song would be sung about the white girl named Katie. Her story would be repeated for generations to come.

Chapter Twenty-One

Meanwhile dawn was breaking, and Carolyn was up early. Her ma and pa had left yesterday to go home to take care of the chores that had been neglected while they were away. Carolyn leaned up against the railing while resting her head against the porch. She had a warm cup of coffee in her hand. Listening, she heard the sound of hoofbeats long before she spotted the riders turning the corner down the road. She knew that five riders had left a couple of days ago, and they should have five riders plus the two girls.

She yelled at her sister, who was coming out right behind her, "Henrietta, come here. I think they're back home."

Henrietta asked as she came up from behind, "Can you see them?"

"I can't tell you who they are, but I can count the horses: two, four and five. I see five horses. Let's hope the girls are with them," she replied with a smile on her face.

As the men rode closer Carolyn's smile slowly disappeared, and she gasped and covered her hand over her mouth. "There are five horses, but only four riders. Marshal Johnson is leading the fifth horse." She took Henrietta's arm.

Henrietta lifted up her dress but half tripped down the stairs in her hurry. "Oh God. Oh my God. Please, not the girls," she mumbled as she reached the bottom step.

Carolyn followed with slower steps. She could make out Charles on his horse and the rest of the men but no Abe or the girls. What was that slung over the last horse's back? She kept thinking she was seeing things. Her stomach started to knot up. The girls weren't with them, and they should be trotting up, not slowly coming down the drive. Something bad had happened.

Charles could see the women as they descended the stairs to greet them. His throat started to close up. It was hard to swallow, and he was trying to be strong.

The men rode up and halted. Marshal Johnson dismounted while his boys just sat on their horses, not making eye contact with anyone. Carolyn was already by Charles's side as he dismounted.

Henrietta, not seeing Abe, ran up to Marshal Johnson.

"Where is Abe? Where is my daughter?" She would not let herself look at that last horse. She wasn't going to look. If she didn't look, it wouldn't be real.

Marshal Johnson looked at Charles. Carolyn was looking at her husband with beseeching eyes. "Where is everyone, Charles? Where are they?" she softly asked.

"Henrietta, there was an accident," Marshal Johnson spoke slowly.

"What are you talking about? Where are my husband and daughter?" Henrietta demanded.

Reid was listening as he came out of the barn. Just as the men were telling the story he stopped and didn't move any further. He could see his aunt run to the last horse screaming, "No! No! Please say it isn't so." His pa was trying to comfort her by telling her that there was nothing that she could do or have done. His aunt swayed a little and her knees buckled as she collapsed to the ground. Reid ran back into the barn.

The bodies were dressed and cleaned, ready for burial.

Amy helped in the house to get everything ready. Doctor Pearson had been summoned to give Henrietta something to calm her down. She now just sat in the chair by the fire, rocking back and forth and not blinking but just staring into the fireplace. Looking around, Amy saw her mother. She didn't look that well, and her father was quite solemn. Everything was moving so fast. The graves had been dug, and Amy could still smell the coolness of the earth—a smell she would never forget when she stood by the deep dark holes. Grandpa and her pa, along with the Johnson brothers, had lowered the boxes into the earth and covered the graves. All that could be seen were two mounds of dirt beneath the oak tree.

Chapter Twenty-Two

Selena woke the next morning as Lone Wolf entered, carrying some breakfast for her.

"Thank you." She took a couple of bites. "I need to go home, Lone Wolf, to see my family. I know that they will be placing Katie and Uncle Abe to rest. I really want to go."

"I will take you." He gave her a dress to wear as she braided her hair, placing a headband on top. Soft moccasins covered her feet, and as they left Laughing Otter and his wife Sweet Owl were coming toward them.

"Hello Selena," Sweet Owl greeted.

"Hello," Selena answered.

"I wanted to tell you that I'm sorry for your loss. I love my husband very much, and his son Rye adores him, as will our little one on the way. We are not to speak the name of a loved one that has passed on. They are now on their journey to the Great Spirit. With the help of many from our tribe we made this for you." She handed Selena two of the most beautiful dream catchers she had ever seen. Looking closer she could tell why—they were made from Katie's long hair.

"How did you get this?" she asked as she accepted the gift.

Sweet Owl answered, "Laughing Otter took it the day the great fire broke out."

"Thank you. I know exactly where I'm going to hang them."

Chapter Twenty-Three

S elena watched as the buggies and wagons went to her old house. She had been right—they were paying their last respects to her family. Lone Wolf walked with Selena to the back side of the barn. They saw the big tall tree and sadly under it two freshly covered graves. Even Pastor Len was there. Everyone was dressed in black. Aunt Henrietta was standing in between Grandpa and Grandma, and Selena could hear her sobbing from where she stood. There were two wooden markers that Grandpa must have helped make last night—he was the carver of the family. Tables had been set, and friends had brought a dish to pass. The women were getting plates ready for the children. The men were huddled together on the far side of the yard.

Lone Wolf had never seen anything like this before. Selena explained each part to him; he thought the custom very strange. Lone Wolf made a bird call every once in a while, and a call would echo back. Little did the mourning crowd know that they were surrounded. Selena didn't know how she was going to get her ma's attention. She didn't want to join them; she wasn't ready for that yet.

Carolyn placed a dish on one of the tables and tucked a stray hair behind her ear. She looked up, sensing that she was being watched, only to see Selena staring right back at her. Before her mother could say or do anything Selena placed her finger to her lips and motioned for her to come over to her. She then stepped back behind the barn wall out of sight once again.

Carolyn tried to act normal as she was talking to a neighboring family, but she only wanted to see her daughter. She moved quietly away; as Charles was surrounded by men, he wouldn't notice her leaving. Carolyn looked one more time behind her as she turned the corner of the barn, running right into Selena.

"Oh Ma." Selena was nearly knocked down but was steadied by her mother.

"Selena." Carolyn held her daughter in front of her, looking her up and down and then pulling her into her arms to give her the biggest hug. "It is so good to see you. Are you okay? Oh my." She wiped a tear from her eye.

Selena hugged her back. She missed the smell of her ma, something she hadn't realized, and she took another big breath. "I'm okay, Ma. I'm not staying long." She looked at Lone Wolf, who up until then had not been noticed. "Ma, I love you all so very much, but I love Lone Wolf as my husband. We will be joined together at the new moon in a couple of days. I will be staying with him." Selena took a deep breath as her mother waited for her to finish. "I know much has happened." She paused for a moment, thinking of Katie. "But one day we will sit down and talk. I just don't want to talk about it right now."

Carolyn nodded her head in agreement and glanced at Lone Wolf.

"Selena, you have been my daughter since you were born and will always be my daughter. You have been a free spirit since the day you were born. By now most of the girls your age have married and have a babe in their arms, but you have never felt that until now, have you?"

Selena nodded her head in agreement.

"Grandma Ellen said you would be coming today. She had tea yesterday afternoon. Once again she is right. She wants you to have something she had been keeping for years. I will be right back."

Selena watched as her mother turned to go into their house. She returned with Pa and a small bundle. Selena hugged her pa and told him how much she loved them all but would remain with Lone Wolf, who was now positioned guardedly behind her, his arms crossed. Charles just looked at him. Carolyn gave her the bundle. Selena motioned to Lone Wolf, who picked up the two dream catchers. She handed them to her ma and pa. "I want you to please hang these in the tree above their graves, Ma. They are made with Katie's hair. She would have liked that; I know she would have."

Carolyn looked at the beautiful dream catchers. "Yes, I will hang them," she replied.

Selena opened the bundle up to find a beautiful white doeskin dress with the most beautiful beadwork she has ever seen along with a matching headband.

Carolyn could see the question on both their faces. "Your great-grandmother was an Indian princess. She had to make the same decision that you are making right now when she met your great-grandfather." Carolyn thought to herself that time has a way of repeating itself, now doesn't it. Her daughter was choosing the life of her great-grandmother. Time would only tell how this story would play out.

Much has happened in the last two years, Selena thought to herself as she rode her horse to her parents' house. She knew this trail by heart. She had wanted to come by herself, but she understood how her husband felt about her going alone, so she always had an escort. The tension had finally eased between her original family and her new one. Her brother Reid had come to the village to visit the most. He had even been given the native name "Rain," because for a while when he first came to visit it would always rain. That brought a smile to her face.

Her aunt Henrietta ended up selling the store to Crazy Pete, who had the money to do so with his gold he had found. He had sobered himself up and turned out to be a very good businessman. Aunt Henrietta still lived there and still cleaned and cooked meals for them both and helped run the store. Selena really thought they would marry one day.

Amy didn't quite understand why or how Selena would ever want to live with Lone Wolf. Once they had shared a room together along with the secrets only sisters shared. They would always be sisters, but there was an unspoken silence that still hovered between them.

Seeing the smoke coming from the chimney of her old home, Selena picked up the pace on her pony. Her mother was always watching out of the window for them, and she was on the porch coming out to greet them.

"Hello Ma." Selena stopped her pony and got off. She placed her daughter down on the ground.

Carolyn watched as her granddaughter took tiny wobbly steps toward her, smiling the sweetest smile she had ever seen. Carolyn bent down while holding out her arms, encouraging her to take her tiny steps. She looked at her—such beautiful brown eyes with dark brown hair that was very long for a toddler her age. Selena had named her daughter correctly.

"Come to Grandma, Katie," Carolyn said.

The End

About the Author

Linda Newton is a small-town girl with big dreams and stories to share with the world. Most of her writing takes place in the hardwoods of the Upper Peninsula, one of the most beautiful places in Michigan. She lives in the U.P. with her two wonderful children, Chad and Rachel, and the love of her life and her biggest fan, her husband Joseph. It has always been a lifelong goal of hers to write a book, and one day she sat down and saw her ultimate destiny unfold right in front of her eyes. With only a single piece of paper and pencil she watched as this story came to life.

Survived by Faith

———◦◦◦❳❲❳◦◦◦———

Amy sat silently in her seat. She could see her reflection in the window as she watched the scenery pass by. She was lost in thought, something she hadn't allowed herself to do in a very long time. This would be the last time she would have to take the long train ride home.

Her wandering mind brought her back in time to that awful summer day and made her forehead wrinkle in worry. It was such a tragedy that day when her cousin Katie passed away violently when Katie's father, Abe, accidently shot her and then took his own life. Her aunt Henrietta had lost her husband and daughter all in one day. Amy narrowed her eyes as the memories came faster. She just could never forgive her older sister, Selena. If it had not been for Selena and Lone Wolf none of this would have ever taken place. How dare Selena then name their half-breed daughter after Katie? Who gave Selena the right to do as she pleased regardless of the consequences?

Suddenly the whistle of the train startled her out of her thoughts. Taking her eyes away from the window, she reminded herself that she wasn't going to do this right now; memories were just that—memories. She was not going to relive the tragedy they had all endured. Reaching down she opened her basket, knowing that she had an apple in there somewhere. Finding it, she took it out, but it slipped out of her hand. She watched as it rolled off her seat and down the aisle until it was stopped by a boot. Looking up she saw a silver star on the coat of a man standing in the aisle. *He must be a sheriff*, she thought.

Reaching down, he picked up the apple and walked over to her. "I believe this belongs to you."

"Thank you," she replied.

"My name is Mathew. Have we met before?" he asked.

Amy looked at him. He did look somewhat familiar, but she didn't have time for such foolishness. "No, we have never met. Good day." She tried to dismiss him.

Mathew was not one to be shrugged off, especially by a pretty lady, and he was a little taken aback. But he loved a good challenge and stood his ground, looking at this prim and proper young lady, who was wearing white gloves, a fitted black dress, and the most unusual hat he had ever seen. The color of the feathers contrasted against the black made the hat stand out. He thought to himself, *She has spirit but is trying to hide it.*

Turning on his charm, Mathew flashed his best smile. It had never failed in the past. "Mind if I sit here? I see that the seat next to you isn't occupied," he asked as he moved closer and started to sit down.

Stuttering, she started to speak. "What? There are plenty of empty seats. There is no need for you to sit in this one." She was quite appalled.

Ignoring her comment, he continued to sit down next to her. "Thank you. My destination is Red Fern Valley; yours?" Mathew asked.

Amy couldn't believe how rude the man was. If he was going to sit there then she was going to move to another seat. She started to get up, but he moved his legs out so she would have to climb over them. Well, two could play at that game. Remembering her apple, she took the most unladylike bite she possible could. Forgetting all of the proper etiquette she had been taught while away at boarding school, she started to chew it noisily and with her mouth open—so much for all she had been taught about being a lady with good manners. Aunt Henrietta wanted to show Amy that there was more to life than farming. Her aunt had offered to send her away to school, and that's where she had been the last four years. *That ought to get him to move,* she thought.

Mathew, not to be outdone, reached into his coat pocket, and Amy watched as he took out an apple of his own. He grinned from ear to ear and, not one to be shown up, took the largest bite he possible could out of his apple. Mimicking her chewing loudly he spoke between bites, "This one is really sweet. Do you want a bite?"

Amy couldn't believe Mathew was making fun of her. Taking a deep breath, she was going to let him have it, until she started to choke on a piece of apple she still had in her mouth. Holding onto her chest she coughed and coughed, trying to catch her breath, until tears ran down her face. Not that it wasn't embarrassing enough to choke in public, the last straw was the way he continued to try to help her by slapping her hard with his hand on her back trying to dislodge the piece of apple. Holding up her own hand in defense, Amy managed to sputter out, "Ouch, don't hit me so hard. I'm okay."

The conductor was now walking down the aisle making his way toward them. "Is there a problem here? Can I help you in anyway?" he asked.

Before she could even answer that she was fine and she was just going to move to a different seat, Mathew spoke first. "No. This pretty lady just choked, that's all, Clint. Don't worry. I'll make sure to keep an eye on her the rest of the ride."

Clint knew he could trust his friend, as they had grown up together, and he tipped his hat at Amy and turned and walked away.

"Excuse me! I am capable of speaking for myself, thank you kindly!" She had fire coming from her eyes.

Chuckling softly, he answered her, "Well now, I beg to differ. It seems to me that you were having trouble eating an apple and trying to speak at the same time. I think you should work on your manners for the rest of the ride home. Where did you say you were going?" he asked.

"I didn't say where I was going. It might be the next stop just to get away from the most annoying man I have ever met—you!"

Shocking her even more, he asked, "You're Amy Williams, aren't you?"

She answered, bewildered, "Yes, but how did you know that?"

It was Mathew who was uncomfortable now, and he clenched his hands into fists that rested on his legs. He decided to change the subject, saying, "I'm the sheriff of Red Fern Valley."

"I know all about the little town of Red Fern Valley. How did you know my name?" She arranged the blanket over her lap as a distraction; maybe she didn't want to know.

Taking his sheriff's hat off, he nervously turned it in his hands and then slowly turned and looked right at her. He didn't need to say anything. His blue eyes and brown hair and the dead seriousness of his expression told her everything she needed to know. He looked just like his pa, Marshal Johnson. It all came rushing back to her. She could see Mathew silently sitting on his horse next to his brother. They had come back to the farm with her father, Charles, and his father along with the bodies of Katie and Uncle Abe. He was Mathew Johnson. Was she ever going to get away from that nightmare?

Watching the different emotions play across her face, he felt unsure of what to say or do. Like she, he had lived with the tragedy. "I'm Mathew Johnson. Amy, are you all right?"

Once again the veil of coolness came over her. "I'm fine," she replied sharply as she turned in her seat to continue to look out of the window.

An awkward silence hovered between them. Both were lost now, deep in their own thoughts.

Mathew broke the silence first. "My father moved away to live in the little town called Hungry Hollow. It's a half-day's ride from Red Fern. Once he left they needed someone to fill his position, so I followed in my father's footsteps. I'm the sheriff there." He pointed to his badge. "I'm on my way back from transporting one of the three Olson brothers. I caught up with him last week. That gang of boys has been causing havoc all over the place. But now there are only two of them left."

Amy continued to ignore him. She was never going to allow herself to have a relationship with any man. She had seen what happened to her sister Selena and was not going down that road—ever. He bumped his elbow into hers, trying to get her attention, "Amy, did you hear me?" he asked.

She did remember something about Mathew. He was someone who wouldn't give up once he had his mind set about something, and that something at the moment just happened to be her. Rolling her eyes, she turned to him with a heavy sigh. "Yes, Mathew, I did hear you. I was trying to enjoy the landscape, but it seems that it is not going to take place this last trip home, with you talking my ear off."

Not to be persuaded since he had her conversing with him, he continued on, "Are you on your way back to your folks' farm? I heard you were away at some fancy school. Is that true?" he asked.

"Yes, I was there but have completed my schooling. I'm traveling back home, but not to the farm. Aunt Henrietta wrote me that the last schoolteacher had married and they were looking to fill the position. I applied, and the town accepted. I will be staying with my aunt and my uncle Pete. They married a couple of years back and continue to run the general store."

They felt the train start to make its transition as it slowed down. They must be close to their destination.

"I guess I will be seeing you around town then, now that you will be living here, right?" Mathew said.

Amy thought to herself, *Not in this lifetime*, but she answered him differently. "I'm going to be really busy with reopening the school. I know it has been closed for a while. I will be busy planning our daily studies. I'm sure between school and visiting my parents I won't have time for anything else."

Taking her off guard, he replied, "That will be just fine. If you need me to accompany you to see your parents I wouldn't mind being your escort. You never know who you are going to run into on the roads nowadays. I will go with you." *Let her think about that one*, Mathew thought to himself.

Amy was at a loss for words. She was thankful for that moment as the train came to a halt. "This is my stop. Would you be so kind as to move over, please? I need to get out."

He stood up, reached down for her basket, and handed it to her. "Do you have other luggage that I can get for you?" he asked.

Amy thought about it. "I do have more bags in another storage car." Mathew and Amy walked down the aisle. Clint was waiting to help her exit down the stairs of the train as he did with the other passengers. Out on the platform the steam let go from the train and blew her hat off. Clint caught it, leaving both men to admire her beautiful blonde hair. Clint handed it over to her, giving her a very big smile.

Searching, she saw her ma and pa. They were smiling and walking toward her along with her aunt.

Carolyn, her mother, walked quickly to her, reaching out to hug her, "Amy, it is so good to see you." She looked at her daughter—what a beautiful young women she had turned into. Charles, her father, hugged her too and then reached for her bags from Mathew.

"Thank you, Mathew. I see that you came in on the train with our Amy."

"Yes, and the pleasure was all mine," he said. "If you will excuse me, I have to be moving on. I have some unfinished business that I need to attend to." He tipped his hat to the ladies, shook Charles hand, and turned and walked to his office located in the jail.

"I have your room all made up for you, Amy," her aunt told her. She was so pleased that Amy had decided to stay with them. "Charles, why don't you carry her bags and we can go over to the house. Then if you want, Amy, we can show you the school and maybe open up some of the windows. Or if you are tired from traveling that can be done another day."

Amy could tell that her mother was hurt about her staying at her aunt's house, but it did make sense—she would be closer to the school by staying in town. She also wouldn't bump into her sister; she would cross that bridge when the time came.

Chapter Two

A my finally had everything unpacked and put away. It was now dark out. She climbed into bed for the night and tried to sleep, but she wasn't quite used to the different room, even if it was Katie's old bedroom. After tossing and turning, Amy slowly drifted off into a light sleep. Suddenly she was awakened with a start—what was that a loud noise? Amy thought she could smell a hint of smoke. Taking a deeper breath, she realized that yes, she could smell smoke. Opening her eyes, she could see an orange glow on the wall coming through her window. Sitting up now and trying to get a better grasp as to what was going on, she thought to herself, *Is it morning already?* Then she heard the frantic ringing of the school bell. Jumping out of bed she headed to the window only to see flames engulfing part of a building located down the road toward the end of town; it looked like it was the church. The commotion outside was crazy. People were running, and others who had come to help were riding their horses. Many folks were starting to carry buckets of water to try to put out the fire. She reached for the clothes she had set out the night before and was dressed in no time. While throwing her shawl on she opened her door and was making her way down the hallway when she ran into her uncle Pete, who was tucking in his shirt.

"The church is on fire!" Amy screamed at him.

"I know. I'm on my way right now," he answered her as Henrietta came up behind him.

Amy watched as her uncle ran down the road to join the other folks who were on their way to help fight the fire. Amy noticed that she was walking way ahead of her aunt, so she slowed her pace down but grabbed her aunt's hand to hurry her along. The air was filled with smoke, and they were greeted with the heat from the fire. The church was engulfed with orange flames that reached out into the night air. Looking through the church windows, she saw that the flames inside were dancing and destroying it, jumping from pew to pew. Amy raised her hand up to protect herself from the glare as well as the heat from the fire—it was unbearable. She watched sadly as the heat guarded the flames so no one could enter to save anything as the fire continued to do its damage. The church would be a total loss.

She saw Mathew barking out orders for folks to get back, away from the burning blaze. She could see two lines of men as they passed empty buckets from one to another until they reached the well. The filled buckets were then passed back hand-to-hand to be dumped on the burning building.

Turning to her aunt, who was watching along with a group of ladies, Amy noticed that she had her hand covering her mouth in disbelief. "I don't think they are going to be able to save the church," she spoke to no one in particular.

"Amy, they are starting to throw water on the schoolhouse. It is closer than you think, and the wind is blowing that way. The sparks could set it on fire too. My goodness, the whole town could go up in flames," Henrietta whispered to her.

Not one to stand still and watch, Amy picked up the hem of her dress and took off running for the schoolhouse. Mathew saw her running and intercepted her as she was going by, reaching out his arm to catch her around her waist and stop her.

"Let me go!" she screamed at him. Panic had set in, "Mathew, let me go. The school—I have to do something for the school!" She struggled against his strong arms.

He shook her none too gently, trying to make her listen. "Stop it, Amy. You are going to get back with the other ladies and let us men take care of this. I don't want you hurt," he yelled back at her.

She looked at him, and as he loosened his grip she took advantage and kneed him in the privates—he let go of her. She broke his grip and continued running down the road toward the school. Mathew was bent over from the blow. *Good thing she doesn't have good aim,* he thought as he shook his head and ran after her. *I should put her over my knee and give her* a *good whipping,* he thought to himself.

Amy stopped running as she came to another fire controlled by a few men who were burning the grass by the school yard.

"Why are they starting another fire? Are they crazy?" She turned to Mathew, who was next to her again and not looking very happy with her. This time he grabbed her by the arm, and he wasn't letting go.

"Amy, it is a firebreak. It should stop the larger fire if it spreads. It won't have anything to burn and will put itself out. Now would you please stay here like a good girl and behave yourself? I have to help with the bucket line. If the flames were to jump or just one tiny spark flew through the air, it could start the school's roof on fire. Promise you will not do anything foolish?"

Amy nodded her head in agreement, and Mathew quickly walked away from her.

Amy decided to do as she was told and stay where she was. Turning around, she saw that the church was now completely engulfed in flames. She took in the scene as it played out before her. Pastor Len had his arms around his wife, Melvina. Amy could see her shoulders shaking from crying. Most folks were standing around, not sure what to do, while others were trying to help put the fire out. She didn't understand the purpose of the line of men passing buckets filled with water. It looked like most of the water was spilled out of the buckets before they reached their destination.

Then something unusual caught her eye. As she looked more closely down the road she spied two men sneaking away from the bank. They had handkerchiefs covering their faces and bags in their hands. She started to walk toward them. Both men were acting very peculiar and not paying any attention to the burning church. *That's very odd*, she thought. *What are they up to?* To get a better look, Amy started walking faster. She passed folks going in the opposite direction of the fire. She watched the two men as they went around to the other side of the bank building. Not halfway to where the men were she watched the two emerge, riding their horses. The men looked to see if they were being watched, and one caught her eye. He pulled back on his reins, and she watched as he said something to the other masked rider. They spoke to each other and then pointed at her, making her stop in her tracks. The taller of the two men gave her the meanest glare she had ever seen, sending a soundless message to her of silence as he pulled out his gun in warning. Amy swallowed hard, looking around her in all directions. *Wasn't anyone else seeing what she was seeing?* The taller one turned his horse and kicked it into motion, and both men galloped out of town. They were gone just like that.

Amy had started back toward the fire when her Aunt Henrietta ran into her. "Child, come with me. It looks like the church is gone and the school is going to be okay. It is almost dawn, and the men are going to be hungry. We are going to make hot coffee and breakfast for everyone, and we need your help."

Amy followed, but she had to tell someone what she seen. "Aunt Henrietta, I saw two men leaving the bank. I think someone robbed it while the fire was being fought."

"Amy, I'm sure the bank is just fine. Why would anyone be in there? It isn't even open. Now come on; we need to get cooking." Her aunt walked off, on a mission.

Amy followed her aunt Henrietta. *Maybe I was seeing things or just confused from all the commotion,* she thought, trying to convince herself. But she shivered as she remembered how the one rider had glared his warning at her. And what about that gun? That wasn't her imagination. *I will tell Mathew when I see him,* she thought.

Amy was given a hot pot of coffee and was filling up empty cups as the men ate their breakfast. It was quite noisy with everyone talking about the fire.

Mathew walked in to get something to eat but stopped in the doorway for a moment. He watched as Amy went from person to person offering to refill empty cups with fresh coffee. He smiled a little. Her blonde hair was braided down her back, but wayward strands had come out, and she kept fighting with them to keep them tucked behind her ear. Her waist was very small and her step light. She spoke kindly to everyone and received an admiring look from time to time. Mathew decided that he wouldn't mind waking up with her each morning. That thought took him by surprise. He wasn't one to become serious— he wasn't ready to settle down just yet.

Amy looked up, and her eyes met Mathew's. He was handed a plate of food, and he made his way to the back of the place. Amy watched as he went to one of the empty tables to sit down. He wasn't looking at her, but she should bring him some coffee. Making her way over, she noticed that he had tried to wash up, but some of the soot was still smeared on the back of his neck.

She approached him, but he continued to eat, ignoring her. "Mathew, would you like some coffee?" she offered.

He lifted his cup up to be filled, saying, "Thank you." Carefully he took a sip and continued to eat his breakfast.

Not sure if she should sit or leave, Amy remembered what she had seen and wanted to tell him. Sitting down next to him, she said, "Mathew, I know you are tired. Do you mind if I sit down? I have to tell you something." He motioned for her to have a seat, but she was already sitting down.

"I don't know if this even means anything, but while the fire was blazing I saw two men come out of the bank," she told him.

That caught his attention, and he put his fork down immediately. "What did you just say?" he asked her.

"I saw two men leaving the bank with bags. They looked to be in a hurry. They got on their horses and rode off quickly." Before she could even finish he was standing up and heading for the door.

Standing up to follow him, she asked, "Where are you going?"

He slowed down to answer her, and at that moment the room just happened to become silent. "I said, to the bank!" Everyone turned to look at them both. Amy left her pot of coffee on the table and took off her apron as she followed him out of the building.

Mathew hurried, and she had to run to keep up with him. They reached the bank steps and walked up. Mathew turned the knob on the door and opened it. "That should be locked," he told her. Walking in, they both heard the sound of glass as it crunched with every step they took.

Mathew motioned for her to stay behind him and then decided differently, "Amy, don't come in any further; stay by the door." He drew his gun out and continued moving cautiously inside.

Amy, only wanting to help, gave him advice from where she stood. "They're not here, I tell you. I saw them leave last night." Amy could tell that he was getting a little angry and that he wasn't listening to her.

Walking back further into the bank, he continued to ignore her. He could see where the window had been broken. The safe door, which should be closed, was open. He stopped where he was—he had seen enough. Retracing his steps back to her he told her, "Amy, I will need you to come with me. I need to get your official statement of what you saw last night. I think I know how the church caught fire—a distraction."

Amy walked out with him. "I told you already what I saw. Can't you just write it down?"

"No, I want an official statement from you. Would you stop being so difficult and for once will you just listen and come with me?" he demanded of her.

Amy was going to argue with him but decided that it had been a long night and all the fight was out of her and continued to walk by his side to his office. "Oh all right, but just for a little while. I need to help the ladies clean up and get to the school to ready it for class."

They entered Mathew's office, and he walked to his desk and sat down with pen and paper. Motioning for her to sit down in front of him, he pointed to a chair. He asked her questions, and she answered as he wrote it all down.

"So what do you think?" she asked him when they were finished.

Leaning back in his chair, he put his hands behind his head. "I think by the description of the two men it could have been the rest of the Olson gang. I just caught the youngest brother the other day, remember? You need to watch yourself, Amy. They don't mess around, and you are the only one who saw them last night."

Amy swallowed hard. "But it was dark out. They wouldn't know who I was, and I wouldn't know them either."

Amy watched as Mathew got up and walked around his desk to sit on the corner of it in front of her and leaned toward her. "I could make sure you were kept safe." He mischievously smiled at her. His gaze was on the bars on the walls of the jail cell, and she followed his look. "I could lock you in one of the cells. You would be safe in there."

Amy stood up quickly as she realized that she had let her guard down again—what was she thinking? Walking away from him, she turned around. "And who would keep me safe from you?" She stuck out her tongue and walked out the door.

Mathew laughed. "That wasn't very ladylike of you," he yelled to her as he shook his head and continued to chuckle. *That Amy, when out of her shell, sure can hold her own.*

CPSIA information can be obtained at www.ICGtesting.com
Printed in the USA
269128BV00002B/117/P